CELTIC MAGIC

DRAGON'S GIFT THE DRUID BOOK 3

LINSEY HALL

For The FireSouls, my awesome friends on Facebook.

1

I crouched in a darkened alley, trying not to breathe in the rank scent of black magic. Despite the cold night air, it somehow smelled fetid and warm. *Gross.*

I seemed to be doing a lot of this lately—crouching in alleys while waiting to launch an attack.

"Do you see anything?" Lavender whispered. She knelt at my right, trying to avoid a puddle of mystery liquid. Normally, Lavender was my nemesis—a fellow trainee at the Undercover Protectorate's Institute of Magic and leader of my *Not-A-Fan* club.

Today, she was my partner, along with Angus, another student. As part of our training, we were here in The Vaults, the most dangerous neighborhood in Edinburgh, about to storm a shop that had been overtaken by Kobolds. The miserable little monsters had set up residence in Madame Mystical's Magical Mementos. Evicting them was our first real-life training exercise.

"It looks empty." I squinted toward the two windows on either side of the shop's door.

The Vaults were underground, and as a result, the street was dark and narrow. Despite the fact that we were far beneath the famous castle in the center of town, a spell made it look like the night stars were shining above.

The Vaults were where most dark magic was created and sold. Maybe the Kobolds thought they could get away with shenanigans down here. That the Undercover Protectorate wouldn't come for them.

They were wrong. We protected everyone, even those who lived on the darker side of town. I loved the mission, and working for the Undercover Protectorate was my dream. But for that dream to come true, we had to succeed and pass this test.

"Are you guys ready?" My heart thundered in my ears.

"Let's do this," Lavender said.

"Cleared for action," Caro said from the back of the alley. She was already a full member of the Protectorate, and she was acting as our supervisor on this test. "Good luck."

"Go!" I said.

As a group, we raced out of the alley and across the street toward the shop. My gaze darted across the shopfront, which loomed three stories tall, carved right into the stone of underground Edinburgh. A light flashed in a second-story window, outlining the figure of a small man. He raised a hand, clearly about to throw some kind of dangerous magic.

"Incoming!" I shouted.

The man in the window hurled a blast of green light at us. I dived right, barely avoiding it as the magic crashed to the ground next to me.

The air shook as the magic detonated, sending shockwaves through my body.

"What the heck was that?" Lavender yelled.

"Bad news!" I sprinted the last few feet to the shop door and yanked it open.

I led the way inside. The shop was three stories tall on the interior, a round open space with bookshelves stretching all the way to the ceiling. Magical objects of all varieties were stuffed onto the shelves, each emitting their own unique magical signature. Dozens of scents and tastes bombarded me.

The space in the middle was empty except for a few glass display cases and some chairs. A ring of low bookshelves surrounded it, creating a walkway around the perimeter of the room. Colorful pixies fluttered near the domed ceiling.

For a moment, I couldn't see any sign of intruders.

"What the hell?" Angus muttered.

"Watch out!" an unfamiliar voice cried.

My gaze darted toward the back of the shop, searching for the woman who had screamed. I spotted her, sitting stock-still between two towering plants. She was tied to a chair. Next to her, the air shimmered.

A Kobold appeared. He looked like a garden gnome, but a heck of a lot meaner. The air continued to shimmer around him, and he grew, shooting up to six feet tall.

"Bloody hell," Angus muttered.

The Kobold threw out his hand, and his magic filled the air. It stank of old garbage and gasoline. Green light burst forth, more of that strange magic that had been hurled at us out in the street.

"Shield!" Lavender cried.

I called on my magic, throwing out my arms to direct my shield toward the oncoming blast. My magic swelled in my chest, strong and fierce. I grinned. My practice with Lachlan had worked.

The magic shot toward my hands, ready to be expelled. But pain tore through me, right at my upper arms.

The magic stopped there.

No shield appeared.

Panic flared as the Kobold's combustive magic neared.

My shield wasn't coming.

I threw myself in front of Lavender and Angus, taking the hit right in the chest. Pain exploded within me as I hurtled back toward the door. I slammed into it as Lavender and Angus scattered, diving for cover behind some of the shorter, free-standing bookshelves.

The Kobold cackled, the sound making the hair on my arms stand on end.

Aching, I scrambled to my feet and dived for cover behind a bookshelf.

What the hell had happened to my magic?

Last night, when I'd gone to the ancient stone circle and learned that I was The Druid Dragon God, two golden tattoos had appeared on my arms. Had they caused this? The magic had swelled out from my chest, going down my arms like normal. But it'd stopped—*right at those tattoos.*

From across the room, a crash sounded. I peered around the edge of the bookshelf. Another Kobold had appeared, this one just as big as the other.

"Come and get it!" he cackled, his voice sounding like a rusty engine.

Lavender leapt up from behind her shelf, her magic shimmered around her. She used her telekinesis to pick up a massive chair and fling it at the monster. The plaid chair hurtled through the air, slamming into the wrinkled Kobold.

A third appeared, close to Angus, who leapt up from behind a shelf and threw a bolt of electricity at him.

My colleagues—I definitely couldn't call them friends—had these two under control, but there was still the one standing guard over Madame Mystical.

I had to get to her. There was no way to tell for sure if all my magic was blocked, but my two other gifts might not come in handy, anyway. My weird premonition and white light magic didn't have much application against Kobolds.

So I crept along the floor, keeping myself behind the bookshelves as I neared Madame Mystical and the Kobold. Crashes and screams sounded from the rest of the shop as Lavender and Angus fought the other two.

I drew a dagger from the ether, gripping the hilt. It was like my version of a comfort blanket. As I crawled past a bowl full of potion bombs, I caught sight of one labeled *Laughing Potion*.

I grabbed it, cradling the red glass ball gently.

"You're doing a shite job, you know!" Madame Mystical screamed.

I peeked around a shelf to judge my distance and shot her a glare. Her red leather catsuit matched her hair, and both gleamed in the light. Her heels were so tall they made my feet hurt just to look at them, but I had to admit that she looked like a particular type of badass.

The Kobold who stood guard over her stared at the fight in the middle of the shop with a confused expression.

Was he counting and realizing I wasn't out there?

Kobolds weren't the cleverest.

Before he could figure it out, I leapt up and threw the potion bomb at him. The glass ball exploded against his chest, sending a bright red liquid splashing over him.

Immediately, he began to shriek with laughter. The sound pierced my eardrums, sending an ice pick through my brain. Madame Mystical's eyes squeezed shut and she twitched.

I raised my blade, trying to focus on the task instead of the pain. I threw the dagger and pierced the Kobold through the chest. He hurtled backward, shrinking down to his original size. He continued to shrivel, disappearing into dust.

Nailed it.

I stood, hurrying toward Madame Mystical. Her eyes widened on something behind me. It was all the warning I got.

Heart thudding, I spun in a circle, just in time to see a fourth Kobold hurl a blast of green magic at me.

I lunged aside, but the blast nailed my legs.

Pain streaked up my body as I slammed to the ground.

"Blöde Kuh!" the Kobold screamed.

What the heck did that mean?

Something told me it was an insult.

Ahead of me, another bowl of potion bombs sat on a low bookshelf. I dragged myself toward it, my legs currently immobilized by the Kobold's explosive green magic.

He thundered toward me, leaping over a chair and dodging a table. I reached for the bowl of potion bombs.

"Get a blue one!" Madame Mystical screamed.

I released the green one and grabbed a blue, rolling onto my back and hurling it at the Kobold. He was nearly to me, towering overhead in his unusually large form.

The glass potion bomb exploded against his chest.

He shrieked, his bulging eyes going wide in his wrinkled green face. He was not *nearly* as cute as Yoda.

In a flash, he froze solid and fell over, then poofed into dust and disappeared.

To my left, Angus climbed unsteadily to his feet. He'd ended up wrestling his Kobold. Thank fates, he'd won.

Lavender strolled over, dusting her hands off and eyeing me. "Why are you on the ground?"

"Uh, the view is better?" Aching, I dragged myself into a sitting position.

"Could one of you come untie me?" Madame Mystical's imperious voice echoed through the room.

"Sorry, Madame Mystical." Angus trotted over.

"Madame Mystical was my grandmother." She twitched an eyebrow, clearly displeased. "*I* am Melusine." Angus untied her and she stood, towering over him in her five-inch heels. "Thank you for rescuing me. The Kobolds showed up yesterday, and they were intent on staying."

I tried dragging myself upward by using the bookshelf, but my legs just wouldn't cooperate. Exhausted and aching, I slid back down against the shelf. I thumped my head back against the it.

Today was really not going my way.

"Drink one of the green potions from that bowl," Melusine said.

"Thanks." I reached behind me and found the potion on the second try. As I swigged it, Caro entered the shop, her platinum hair gleaming.

"Well done, you three! A record." She grinned widely.

"No thanks to Ana," Lavender muttered. "Her shield went out."

I thumped my head back against the bookshelf again. *Of course.*

"She did take out two of the Kobolds." Melusine's gaze met mine. "You're Ana, I assume."

"I am." My legs tingled, and I winced.

"You should be good to walk now," Melusine said.

I dragged myself upright, then took a few unsteady steps.

Melusine was already stalking around the shop, her red catsuit gleaming under the light as she began to clean up.

"Do you need any help?" Angus's voice was hopeful, and I was pretty sure that he wasn't thinking about cleaning.

"No, I'll use magic," Melusine said. "Thank you again. You can go now."

I met Caro's wry grin and shrugged. That was that.

As a group, we left the shop, heading out into the dark night. I stuck near Caro, since she actually liked me. The feeling was mutual. The water mage was one of my favorite people at the Protectorate.

"We really did it in record time?" I asked as we walked down the darkened street. It was a narrow cobblestone affair that wound down through the town, past dark little shops and crowded bars. Gas lamps flickered at doorways, and various faces peered out at us, suspicious.

"You did," Caro said. "Jude will be pleased."

"Good." Top of my list was making Jude happy. As the leader of the PITs—the Paranormal Investigative Team—and hopefully my future boss, I wanted her to think I was good at this.

But with my magic on the fritz...

I shoved the thought away. I'd have to address it, and soon, but right now, I just wanted to get out of The Vaults. It was a creepy place, like the darker side of a fairy tale, and being underground just felt weird.

Caro led us out of The Vaults and through the magical bookshop that acted as the secret entrance. A special golden stone was the ticket through the bookshop and into The Vaults, but it didn't make the ornery bookshop actually *like* you.

"Don't let the door hit you on the way out," a crotchety old voice said. It sounded like it belonged to a 102-year-old woman with a serious case of attitude, but it was actually the house itself speaking.

"Love you, too!" Caro shouted. "Always a delight to visit."

"Stuff it up your nose!" The house harrumphed.

I grinned as I stepped out onto the main street in the Grass-market, the supernatural district of Edinburgh. Immediately, the air tasted fresher, and the morning sky was a welcome change from the fake one in The Vaults.

It didn't take us long to make our way down the street and through the special portal that would take us back to the High-lands, where the Protectorate castle sat on a lonely piece of land overlooking the sea. Once I stepped through the glowing portal, the ether sucked me in and spit me out in the Enchanted Forest.

From there, the fairy lights led us between the twisted old trees, down a path toward the castle.

When we appeared on the main lawn, the enormous stone structure beckoned. Towers reached toward the sky, and the windows glittered in the early morning sunlight.

"I love it here," Caro said. "It's been five years, and I'm still not used to it."

It'd only been a couple months for me, and I couldn't help but agree. I'd never get used to this place. In the distance, the Cats of Catastrophe chased the Pugs of Destruction across the lawn. Princess Snowflake III led the charge, her long white fur blowing in the wind. Muffin kept pace, but as usual, Bojangles was chasing his tail. The orange cat was the epitome of a sweet moron, but I loved him. And damn, could he fight.

The Pugs of Destruction glowed blue, the little ghosts leading the cats on a lightning-fast chase. Mayhem, the pug with wings, kept flying back to bark at Snowflake, then turning around and darting away.

"I don't think the cats will ever catch them," Caro said.

"Not sure what they'd do with them if they did," I said. "They're ghosts."

Though Muffin, the Cat Sìth, was so magical he might be able to manage something, he had too good a heart to hurt the pugs.

"Hey!" Bree's voice sounded from across the lawn.

I turned, spotting her coming out of the stable where we stored the buggy, our monster truck and my pride and joy. She had a black grease stain on her cheek and a big smile on her face.

"Hey." I grinned as she joined us. "How's it going?"

"Good. Just had a bit of time so I thought I'd give the buggy a tune-up. How are you?"

She asked the question just as my gaze was drawn toward

the stone circle that sat near the sea. The enormous stones jutted toward the morning sky, and magic glowed around them.

The circle had always called to me before—and repelled me at the same time, which was weird—but it had never glowed like that.

"Ana?" Bree poked my arm.

"Oh, sorry!" I turned to her. "Distracted."

"Yeah. I can tell. By what?"

Caro had gone off to join Lavender and Angus, so it was just me and my sister. I rubbed my arm where the new tattoo had sunk into my skin and eyed the stone circle again.

"Ana? You're making me nervous. What's up?"

"Something's wrong. Last night, I stepped into the stone circle." I hadn't seen Bree since then. "A super powerful godly voice told me that I'm The Druid."

Her eyes widened with excitement. "You're the Celtic Dragon God?"

"Looks like it." It should be pretty cool. I didn't know much about the Celts, though I'd managed to do a quick search in the library. Hadn't pulled up much since the records were sparse, but I'd learned a bit. "But I also got two new tattoos."

"What!?"

"Not at a tattoo parlor or anything." I liked to switch up my style choices too much to get tattoos that were permanent. I showed her the tattoos. "I got them while I was in the circle. Glowing, golden Celtic knots. They wrap around my upper arms."

"That sounds badass."

"They look cool, yeah. But I just tried to use my magic for the first time, and they *stopped* it. Like, the magic couldn't flow from my chest and out of my hands."

Bree glanced up. "Oh crap."

"Exactly. Something is really wrong, and I have no idea what."

She squeezed my arm. "We'll figure it out."

We'd finally arrived at the courtyard that led up to the castle, so I zipped my lips, not wanting to talk about my now-faltering magic since Jude might be nearby. I'd *just* gotten a bit of control, thanks to Lachlan's help. The fact that it was on the fritz was no good.

Together, we climbed the wide steps. The massive wooden doors swung open, revealing the huge entry hall with a soaring ceiling.

Normally, it was a quiet part of the castle, with people passing through on their way to other destinations. This time, however, there were three figures standing in the middle. Two wore long white robes, while the third was dressed in old-fashioned leather armor.

Scratch that.

It wasn't old-fashioned looking. It was positively ancient. Her red hair was tied on her head in a variety of crazy knots, and the sword at her side had a beautiful twisted iron hilt.

The two who wore the robes were talking a mile a minute at Jude, whose brows were halfway to her hairline.

Bree grabbed my arm, and we stopped stock-still, not wanting to disturb them.

And who were we kidding? We also wanted to eavesdrop.

We tucked ourselves against the door, in plain sight—I wasn't about to go sneaking around and get myself in trouble—but we were out of the way enough that we wouldn't disturb them.

"I recognize her," Bree whispered. "The one with the red hair."

"Who is it?"

"Maira. She's a Celt."

"Whoa." Could that be a coincidence?

"I met her when I was in the Celtic god Cocidius's realm. She was a captive."

"Not anymore."

"No, I helped free them all."

I grinned. "'Course you did." It was just the kind of thing that Bree would do.

I strained my ears to hear what they were saying. Both of the figures in robes were men, and the tallest one was speaking. "I'm telling you, the dark magic is unlike any we've ever seen. It's unrivaled in its devastating nature."

"And you say that it broke into the Otherworld?"

Otherworld. That was the Celtic afterlife, the realm of the gods and the dead.

"Just yesterday," the tall figure said. "It broke right through the circle at Caernavon. I don't know how it managed—it should have been impossible. But it made it through. Now it's cutting through our realm, leaving a terrible trail of destruction in its wake. It's *destroying* Otherworld."

"And you say you need help tracking it?" Jude asked.

"Yes, precisely. This is where the druidic seers said that we would find the help we need."

"You've come to the right place. We have just the team for the job."

As if they sensed me, the two robed figures turned and looked right at me. Then they pointed.

"We want her," they said in unison.

Oh fates.

"Bree?" Jude asked. "She's new to the Paranormal Investigative Team, but she's very talented."

"Not her," Maira, the warrior, said. "Though she is very talented and I owe her my life. The elders are speaking of The Druid. There's no doubt that she's the one meant to help us."

"Yes," the tall figure said. "We want The Druid Dragon God."

Welp—they knew what I was.

I'd been keeping that pretty close to the vest. Only trusted members of the Protectorate knew that I was a Dragon God. They were the only ones who had any reason to know. But Bree was the only one aware that I was The Druid.

Now these random strangers knew?

It had to be because they were Celtic and had some extra insight, but I still didn't like it.

Jude's brows jumped all the way to her hairline this time. If they could have, they'd have jumped right off her head. Her starry blue eyes met mine. "The Druid?"

I hadn't had a chance to tell Jude about my visit to the stone circle. Between sleep and class and popping into the library to do a bit of reading about it, I'd been busy.

This was not how I'd anticipated this going down.

"Yeah." I nodded. "Last night I learned that I'm The Druid."

Bree was The Valkyrie. I was the Druid. And I was all kinds of confused.

"That's new," Jude said.

I nodded. "Very."

"Did you know that some distressed Celts would show up on our doorstep begging for your help?" she asked.

"Nope." I looked at the Celts. There was reverence in their eyes, or something like it. Well, the two robed ones, at least. Maira just grinned at me and Bree.

To say that I was more comfortable with the grin than I was with the reverence was an understatement.

"Am I interrupting something?" Lachlan's voice sounded from behind me.

My heart went wild and my brain went on the fritz.

I turned. He met my gaze, and something passed between us. Heat, definitely. I felt like a wire connected us, and someone had just plucked it like a guitar sting. The tension vibrated in the air. Our kiss played through my mind, and I probably looked totally zoned out.

I shook myself. He shot me a small half smile, then looked at Jude.

I sucked in a slow breath, trying not to be a totally awkward dork, and turned from him.

Seriously?

This was his timing?

I was confused as hell and overwhelmed, and the object of my affection/lust chose this moment to show up and add a bit of sexual tension and mild panic to the mix? Last night, we'd *just* agreed to not ignore our feelings. Apparently, I hadn't had enough time to chill out about it and become a normal person.

"I think we need to go to the round room," Jude said. "This qualifies as round-room big-deal discussion material."

No kidding.

2

I trusted Lachlan, I didn't object to him coming with us to the Protectorate's version of a war room. The Celts seemed pleased to be upgraded to the medieval-style room where we discussed the most important issues at hand. They settled in at the big round table as if they visited every day for tea.

Unfortunately, I didn't have too much else to say about being The Druid and the possible savior that these people were looking for. I'd have *liked* to have more information about my situation, but I just....*didn't*.

The one thing I didn't mention was that my magic was on the fritz because of the tattoos. I didn't want to give Jude any reason to think I wasn't capable of being at the Academy and passing with flying colors. Quickly.

"You insist that Ana is the only one who can help?" Jude said.

The three of them nodded.

"She's the reason we came here," Maira said.

"Isn't the timing a bit weird?" I asked. "I just discovered that I'm The Druid, and now you're here, needing my help."

"You were fated for this," the shorter man said. "I am Owyn, and I am an elder druid. Not *The* Druid, like you. But I have visions and prophecy. I can see this."

Vision and prophecy.

Just like I had.

I'd wondered where that new magic had come from, but apparently it was a druid thing.

"What are druids, exactly?" I asked. I'd gotten a definition in the library, but it'd been vague.

"We perform a number of functions, but primarily we are the knowledge holders of the Celts. We can act as lore-keepers, seers, religious leaders, healers, and legal authorities. We also protect the magic of the Celts," Owyn said.

Healers. The white light that had helped heal me.

That new power was starting to make sense, too.

These guys definitely had answers for me. I knew almost nothing about the Celts, and I certainly knew almost nothing about my new magic. Info in the library had been sparse on this subject, primarily because the Celts had utilized an oral method for passing down history and information.

If you wanted knowledge about them, you had to go to the source.

And these guys were the source.

"I want to help." I looked straight at Jude. "I can do this."

Her gaze moved between the druids and me. A thousand thoughts flashed in her mind, clearly.

"You aren't fully trained," she said.

"Neither was Bree when she set off to the Norse realm to learn about her magic," I said.

Bree nodded. "True story."

"I know," Jude said. "That was dangerous, but necessary. So is this. The other division heads have been chafing at the idea of new recruits being given so much freedom—it's one of the reasons I've been harder on you, Ana. Our rules have kept us safe and alive for hundreds of years. But I agree that this is important. And it's a double standard to let Bree go but deny you."

"And we need her help," Owyn said. "Desperately."

"And I want to learn more about what I am," I said. "They can teach me."

"We will," Owyn said. "There are things she can gain in Otherworld. Things she *must* gain. It's only natural that she go. She can help us with our problem while learning about what she is. The fates have decreed that it must be done." His voice rang with passion.

"You have more magic than you did when you came here," Jude said. "That will help protect you."

I kept my face blank as I nodded. Bree didn't breathe a word, and fortunately Angus and Lavender weren't there to report on my dismal performance back at Madame Mystical's.

"I'll go," Lachlan said. "As backup."

Next to him, Owyn grinned, delighted. The old druid liked something about this.

Jude's eyes moved toward him. "Um, all right?" She leaned forward. "You don't work for us, you know."

A grin tugged at the corner of his mouth.

Damn, that was sexy. He looked like such a rake. I'd borrowed a few of Caro's old romance novels the other week, and he fit the definition perfectly. Just looking at him made my heart race.

"I'm aware," Lachlan said. "But I'd like to help with this."

Jude's gaze moved from me to Lachlan, understanding clearly dawning. "Ah, right. Well, it's not my place to say no. You're powerful and she could use the help. The protection."

"I can protect myself." I frowned.

Jude grinned. "Good. I know that. It's why you're here. You're tough, Ana. I don't doubt you. But it's always good to have backup. And Lachlan is good backup."

That was the truth.

Owyn leaned forward. "He has a role to play, actually. An important one. So this is perfect."

"I do?" Lachlan asked.

Owyn nodded. "Indeed. There will be a battle for you alone."

He grinned. "Perfect. Any hints?"

"Unfortunately, no. But I have seen in the fire that a large and powerful shifter mage must accompany the Druid. That must be you."

Lachlan nodded.

"It's settled, then," Jude said. "Ana, you'll be going to Otherworld to help them with the dark magic. I'll run interference with the other departments. They'll be annoyed, but they'll have to deal."

"Thank you." I turned to the druids. "Let's go kick some dark magic butt."

Lachlan and I departed almost immediately, following the Celts back toward the front entry of the castle.

Maira, who clearly acted as the Druid's bodyguard, walked alongside Bree, catching up. I stuck close to Lachlan, leaning in to whisper, "Thank you for coming."

"I wouldn't miss it." He squeezed my hand, and a shiver raced up my arm. I hadn't seen him since last night, when we'd agreed to not pretend there was nothing between us. I didn't know where it would go from here, but I wanted to find out.

Not to mention, I wanted to find out his reason for denying the attraction and using the lame excuse of "we work together." I'd asked him, but he'd sidestepped the question.

We stepped through the main doors of the castle and out into the early morning air. It was late winter, brisk and cool with snow scattering the ground. It must have fallen while we were in the round room. I sucked in a deep breath, enjoying the icy sea scent of the air.

Bree, who'd been in front of us, turned and hurried to me, catching my eye. "Be careful, okay."

"You know me."

"Yeah, Miss Plan A, B, and C. But oftentimes, those plans involve you throwing yourself into danger."

"You know I can handle it." I hugged her.

"I know," she muttered against my hair. "But I also know what happened when I visited the Norse realm, and it wasn't pretty. I can't imagine the Celtic one will be any better. So be careful."

I pulled back and met her gaze. "I will. Promise. And take care of Rowan."

"Always." She smacked a kiss on my cheek, then hurried back into the castle.

Maira turned to us. "We'll take a transportation charm back to the portal at the stone circle. We'll use that to enter Otherworld."

I nodded, excitement welling in me.

These were my people.

Or at least, I was one of them. There was a difference, somehow. Because I already had my people. Bree, Rowan, and the Protectorate. But that didn't mean I didn't want to know about these folks as well. To become part of something that was tied to my past and my present.

Maira dug into a leather pouch attached to her waist and withdrew a transport stone. She hurled it to the ground, where it exploded in a cloud of silvery dust.

She held out her arm. "After you."

The two Druids led the way, and I followed, letting the ether suck me in. It pulled me through space, making my head spin, and finally spat me out in a wide, open field. The air was bitter cold here, but there was no snow on the ground. I turned, feeling magic that tugged at my chest.

When I spotted a huge stone circle, I stopped.

Bingo.

The source of the magic. And the portal to Otherworld.

Excitement shivered across my skin as I looked at it.

I'm really going there.

The Druids were watching me with a combo of interest, awe, and skepticism—which was pretty weird. I turned from them, spotting Lachlan as he stepped through the portal. I was glad he was here—not just as backup, but as moral support, too.

Finally, Maira appeared, and we started toward the stone circle.

She sidled up next to me, which was good. I'd rather ask her my questions than the other two. I might be *The* Druid and these two guys might be druids, but the warrior Maira was more on my level.

"So, stone circles act as portals to Otherworld?" I asked.

"Sometimes, along with other things. The Celts didn't build the circles—they were here long before we were. But we use them for different purposes. Other things can be portals too. But usually it's symbolic places like this."

Symbolic was right. The majesty of the stones that towered toward the sky took my breath way. No wonder the Celts had reused the stone circles. They were amazing. I'd been entranced by the one back at the castle, but this one was even bigger.

"This one leads to an entrance close to our Oppidum," she said. "But there are many others that lead to different places in Otherworld. It's huge."

"What's an Oppidum?" I asked.

"Walled city." She grinned. "You'll see."

Magic pricked against my skin as we neared the stones. They were jagged, uneven things, very tall but skinny. I could almost see the power sparking on the air.

"Just step in," Maira said. "You're a Celt, so it will recognize you and allow you entrance to Otherworld. If you hold Lachlan's hand, he can go, too."

I reached for Lachlan's hand, unable to stop my smile when his large palm closed around my own. The druids stepped between the stones and disappeared right into thin air. Maira waited, no doubt for us, so I followed, Lachlan at my side.

Just like with a normal portal, the ether sucked me in and threw me across space. Except there was a little something extra here—a tugging that I felt deep in my middle as my head spun. When I appeared on the other side, I stumbled, gripping Lachlan's hand tightly.

We stood in the middle of an identical field, but in the distance, a black stain spread across the land. It looked like tar or oil.

The scent wafted toward me, reeking of garbage and despair. I wrinkled my nose.

Maira appeared next to me. Her gaze went immediately to the black stain. "That is what you are here to stop."

"And you have no idea what it is?" It stretched for miles, like a snake that slithered off into the distance, poisoning everything it touched.

"No idea what it is. Just that it reeks of evil and is killing anything it touches. It goes farther and farther. We assume it is following whatever intruder is making their way through Otherworld."

"I'll stop them." Anger and determination heated my chest. This was my home, in a sense. Nothing would hurt my home.

I turned from the stain, unable to look at it any longer, and spotted a hill that rose toward the sky. Three circular shaped walls surrounded the top of the hill. Each ring of wall was on a different level of the hill, gradually rising upward.

"That's the Oppidum," Maira said.

"Who are you defending against? Isn't this the Celtic Other-world? You shouldn't have enemies here." That was the problem —the invaders that I was here to hunt were the *only* enemies.

"The walls aren't for defense," Maira said. "Though they could serve as that in a pinch. They're more of a status symbol. They help us control trade and maintain power."

"Cool." I let go of Lachlan's hand and started toward them, desperate to see inside.

The druids followed behind, silent. They gave off the air that I'd always associated with monks. Quiet contemplation and power in knowledge. Maira led us to the city.

I couldn't help but think of my mother, who'd arrived in the stone circle to stop me from discovering this information. She'd said it was deadly—to me.

Maybe that was so, but I was desperate to learn about who I was. I'd never turned back from a challenge. And these people needed me.

We reached the hill, which soared high above, and began to climb, passing one ring of wall and then another. The first two gates had been left open for us, and there were no guards at the towers on either side.

As we neared the main gate at the top, I began to hear the noises of a city. Voices, animals, the sound of cart wheels creaking.

"This is amazing. Like stepping back in history." I turned to Maira. "What year is it here?"

"2018 AD, I suppose, just like Earth. Time passes here as well, but slightly differently. We maintain the ways of our past, so it looks like we're somewhere in the first millennium BC. But this city—this whole realm—is an amalgamation of the many types of Celtic beliefs and styles."

"It'd give an archaeologist a heart attack, you mean," Lachlan said.

"Exactly. Good thing none of those grave robbers are here." Maira grinned. "Celts aren't just one religion. We are a group that shared a culture and a way of living. We existed for thousands of years, spread across Europe, from Spain to Turkey and all the way up to Scotland. You'll see that in Otherworld—all of our people are here, all of them living in different ways with different beliefs."

I liked that idea—they might be different, but they were united.

We stopped in front of the last wall that protected the city. This main gate was closed, and it began to creak loudly as it rose to permit us entrance. Two guards at the top of the twin towers wore leather armor like Maira's. They waved down, big grins on their faces.

As we stepped through, I was struck by the sheer enormity of the place.

It was a city.

True, it was built of wood and there were no skyscrapers, but it was huge. Maira led us past an area of round houses with thatched roofs, toward long low buildings that looked like many people could live within.

Finally, we reached a part of town that looked like it contained large estates. The patches of land were larger, as were the buildings.

"Where are we going, exactly?" I asked.

"To meet someone." Maira grinned enigmatically. "There is a lot you must learn."

She led us up the path to one of the large wooden buildings. Goats and sheep grazed in the yard out front. We'd neared the door of the house when a woman rushed out.

I stumbled, nearly going to my knees.

"Mom?" I felt lightheaded.

She rushed up to me, blond hair glinting in the light and her green dress billowing about her legs. She threw her arms around me.

It felt like the comfort of a million hugs. The million hugs I'd missed out on when she'd died.

Tears sprang to my eyes as I hugged her back, my mind spinning. What the heck was happening?

She pulled back, grinning. "I can't believe you're here. Look at how big you are!"

I blinked, struggling to take it all in. The last time I'd seen her alive, I'd been thirteen. She'd told us to run while she held off the ones who hunted us.

She'd succeeded, but it had killed her.

"What are you doing here?" I asked.

"This is my afterworld," she said. "My ancestors were Celts. Like you. And because I am a seer, I came here upon my death."

I couldn't believe it. I was really with my mother. And she was solid. A real person. Not a ghost like when she'd appeared in my dream at the stone circle, telling me that I must not pursue my identity.

"Did you really come to me in a dream and try to stop me from learning what I am?" I asked.

She nodded.

Maira cleared her throat, and I jumped.

My mother flicked her an annoyed glance. "Fine, Maira.

You're right." She looked at me. "We need to go to the sacred grove. I'll explain on the way."

"All right." I had no idea what was happening, but I was willing to go along to find out.

I turned, following my mother back down the lane, away from her house. The two druids had disappeared, but Maira stuck by our side. Lachlan held back, as if he sensed I wanted space with my mother.

I did.

I liked Lachlan. A lot. But this was some intensely personal stuff, and we weren't there yet in our relationship. Not at that level of sharing, at least.

Maira led us toward the back of the village.

"Well?" I asked my mom. "What happened in the dream?"

"My own selfishness." She sighed. "This is dangerous, Ana. What you are here to do. What you will learn about yourself. When you become The Druid and embrace all your powers... it is very likely that you could die." Distress creased her face.

"You've seen this in a vision?" I asked.

"I see many futures. And that is one of them. Many of them, actually. There are many ways that this could go wrong. And I wanted to protect you, so I tried to keep you from learning what you are. But that is no longer possible."

She'd seen a vision of me dying? I swallowed hard. Yikes. "You've always tried to protect us."

"Always." She gripped my hand, her voice fierce. "But I can't protect you from yourself. From what you are meant to be. I've accepted that. All I can do is try to help you."

I smiled, gratitude welling within me.

Maira led us through a back gate and down the side of the hill. In front of us, a procession of figures in white and green robes was heading toward a forest about a mile away.

"Who are they?" I asked.

"Druids," my mother said. "Now that you are here, we will perform a ritual to ask the oak trees for help with your mission. We know that you are the one meant to stop the evil encroachers, but we don't know *how* exactly. We hope that they will guide us."

"Sounds good to me." Because I had no idea how to stop that black stain besides finding and killing the one who created it. Maybe that would do the trick.

We followed the druids down the hill and toward the forest. As we neared the enormous oak trees, something in my chest calmed. It felt like I was meant to be here. Like I'd waited my whole life to come to this place.

And finally, I had.

We passed through the trees, which rose tall on either side, their leaves rustling in the breeze.

"Oaks are sacred," Maira said. "We come here for all of our most important rituals."

She led us toward a small clearing where a massive bonfire had been built. Though it was daylight, it was mostly dark back here. The canopy of oak leaves cut off much of the sun, and fairy lights sparkled among the trees.

A dozen druids surrounded the fire, both men and women. They were dressed in long cloaks of different colors, and many of them wore headdresses. Their gazes were solemn as they looked at me, and suddenly, I felt the weight of their expectations heavy on my shoulders.

A woman who wore a headdress of antlers stepped forward, her white dress gleaming in the light of the fire. "Welcome, Ana Blackwood, Warrior Druid."

I nodded and stepped forward. Apparently, this was happening.

Lachlan held back, but I could feel his gaze on me, giving me strength.

"You are here to learn about your power," the woman said. "To become The Druid, fully."

I nodded. "And to stop whatever evil is spreading across this land."

"Your fate is entwined with it." She gestured toward the fire. "Step closer. Be enveloped by the sacred smoke."

My mind was racing, but I did as I was told. When the druids had said that I was meant to come here, they'd meant it. They even had a ritual all set up and ready for me. And if my mother trusted them, then I did, too.

I stepped close to the flames, until I could feel the heat flickering on my face. Within the dancing orange fire, I caught sight of a familiar shape.

A cat made of fire.

A hairless cat. A jewel glinted at its ear.

Muffin.

The Cat Sìth was here, watching over me. And, apparently, he could turn into fire.

Around me, the druids began to chant. Their low voices flowed through the forest. The smoke rolled toward me, pale gray and thick. It enveloped me, but it wasn't difficult to breathe.

Magic stole through my body, making my muscles tremble. Visions flashed in my eyes. Battles and blood, victory and defeat. Life and death.

In the distance, the sound of chanting rose, filling the air with the power of a thousand voices. My head spun as the visions came faster and faster. I couldn't make sense of them. None of them stuck around long enough for me to really see them. They were more a feeling than anything else.

Lightning struck in the distance, thunder cracking behind it.

The smoke disappeared.

The visions faded.

I stumbled backward, gasping. The fire in front of me had died down, and the circle of druids stared at me.

"What just happened?" I asked.

The woman wearing the antlers spoke. "We druids are the holders of knowledge. We are the teachers, judges, healers, priests, seers. We use the flame to help see the future and the present—to determine courses of action that must be taken."

"And that's what just happened?"

She nodded. "You are the Warrior Druid, Ana. You are the only one among us with the power and ferocity to be the warrior. The Celtic gods have blessed you with their magic, but you must obtain their gifts."

"How do I do that?"

"The smoke has revealed that you must go on a dangerous journey of knowledge to the sacred grove," the antlered woman said. "Your path will interlace with the evil that has invaded this land. The smoke has indicated that the evil takes a path that is entwined with yours. It may also seek knowledge from the grove."

"So if I go there, I can learn more about my magic and also about the one who is invading Otherworld."

"Yes. You are linked."

Oh boy. I didn't like the sound of that.

"You have tools at your disposal," the woman said. "Your tattoos are a sign of the Warrior Druid. They are a powerful weapon, but you must unlock them. You will find something at the grove to help with this."

"Any idea what?" I asked.

"That is for you to find out."

"How do I find the grove?"

"Your premonition sense will guide you. It is one of a druid's greatest gifts—the ability to see the truth. To see what must be done. Consider it your druid sense."

The corner of my mouth cocked up. My druid sense. I liked that.

"I'll get started right away," I said.

"Good. But be forewarned. It will be dangerous."

"I'd be surprised if it weren't."

3

An hour later, I said goodbye to my mother and the druids and set off with Lachlan. My mother had given Lachlan a leather backpack full of food for the journey, and Maira had given us two white horses, each wearing a simple leather saddle and bridle. I'd never ridden a horse before, and this one seemed to realize I was an idiot. He looked at me with a pitying expression that made me feel better, frankly. He'd go easy on me.

I hoped.

"You can call him Stan," Maira said. "He'll take you as far as he can, then he'll return home."

I patted the side of Stan's neck, and he gave me a baleful look. Lachlan seemed much more at ease on his mount, which was named Finn.

We set off, riding across the field toward the black stain that snaked over the ground. Fortunately, Stan was as nice as he looked, and he kept his pace even and easy.

As we neared the black stain, it began to stink of death and decay.

"What kind of magic is this?" I peered down at the blackened grass that appeared to be rotting. The stain was about twenty feet wide, but seemed to be very slowly growing.

"I've no idea." Lachlan frowned. "But don't touch it."

"You don't need to tell me twice."

The sun rose higher in the sky, warming the day and gleaming on the green grass that hadn't been destroyed by the dark magic. Birds chirped in the distance, cheerful songs that didn't match the worry that tugged at my chest.

But beneath the worry was a sense of knowing—like I was home. And that same sense drew me forward, toward the east, where answers would lie. Though my magic was on the fritz, my premonition sense was going strong. It was the druid in me, more so than anything else, telling me to keep going east. It followed the path of the dark magic that cut across the land like a horizontal lightning bolt.

"The dark magic has to be following whoever invaded this place," I said. "Like they're so evil they leave a slime trail behind."

"Like a giant slug?" Lachlan grinned.

"Exactly."

I expected to see a forest eventually, but the path stayed clear, a flat meadow that went on endlessly. An hour later—which is a *very* long time on a horse for a newbie—the terrain ahead became rockier. I squinted.

"Does it look like the land just drops off ahead?" I asked. "Right after the rocks."

"Aye. A giant ravine, maybe."

I rode up to the edge of it, slowing Stan as we neared. He looked back at me, pinning me with one eye as if to say, "You seriously think I'd walk off a cliff?"

I shrugged. "Sorry."

He neighed, and I took it as an acceptance of my apology.

Lachlan jumped off his horse and tied the reins off to a large, slender rock. I did the same, then approached the huge gorge. It dived down into the earth at least a hundred feet. It was even wider across, with no bridge in sight.

"Well, this is going to slow us down." I looked at Stan, who didn't seem inclined to leave. Since Maira had said he would just leave when he was done helping us, I assumed it meant we had to get him across the ravine with us. I looked back at Lachlan. "Any idea how to get across?"

He was studying our surroundings, his brow creased. "Not yet."

I turned, inspecting the giant stones that surrounded us. They were totally different than the rest of our surroundings, and sparkled with a light layer of magic. A pile of glassy looking rocks sat to my right, with another pile farther back.

I pointed to them. "Those are weird."

Lachlan approached the pile and picked up a rock, inspecting it. "Aye. Iron slag, I think."

"Slag?"

"A byproduct of iron production. Slag can be used in some spells. The more ancient, the better."

Iron production? Out here?

I stood on a huge rock slab. It was indented with a long channel that looked like a gutter, and the whole thing vibrated with magic. Water could flow through the channel and over the edge of the cliff. I followed the channel back to the tall rocks that sat about ten yards from the cliff edge.

Up close, it appeared to be some kind of strange setup. A pile of logs and kindling sat beneath a huge bowl-shaped rock that was propped between two boulders. Next to it was another pile of stones, each streaked through with different colors.

"We're someplace strange." I picked up one of the gray-streaked stones. "If those rocks over there were slag, then this is probably iron ore."

Lachlan approached the huge bowl-shaped rock that was propped over the long-dead fire. "And this is a crucible."

"The Celts were an Iron Age people, right?" I looked around with new eyes. "This must have been a forge."

"Outside?"

"There might have once been a building over it, but maybe not." I pointed to the crucible. "Once the iron was molten, they'd tip this over, and the liquid would flow down the channel toward the gorge. Maybe it would then form a bridge."

"There's magic here," Lachlan said. "It'd be necessary for that plan to work."

A meow sounded from behind me. *Light it up!*

I turned, spotting Muffin sitting on a rock. Bojangles and Princess Snowflake III sat next to him.

I looked at Lachlan, who shrugged. "Might as well try."

I pulled a box of matches from my pocket and knelt by the logs and kindling.

"You always carry matches?" Lachlan asked.

"Got to be prepared." It was a little thing—me being prepared for this random challenge—but it made me grin.

I struck the match and held it to the kindling. As soon as the tiny flame sparked, magic swelled in the air. The fire burst to life, and I stumbled backward.

The flame roared, growing ten feet tall, then fifteen. It totally encompassed the huge crucible.

Lachlan grabbed my shoulders and dragged me backward, away from the heat. I scrambled upward, my heart pounding.

We watched as the heat grew. Finally, the crucible tilted over, pouring molten iron into the channel that cut through the ground. From twenty yards away, the horses watched with bored expressions.

"I guess they're used to this," I said.

"I'm not." Lachlan watched as the molten metal flowed toward the gorge. When it reached the edge of the rock, it rose up in the air, forming a narrow bridge that began to stretch across the ravine. Magic sparked more strongly in the air as the metal flowed. I grinned.

It didn't take long for the bridge to form, and within minutes, the molten metal hardened into a dark gray iron bridge.

"Wow." I turned to Lachlan. "Ready to cross?"

"Let's do it." He strode to his horse and untied the reins, then swung himself up into the saddle.

I joined him, and our mounts trotted toward the bridge like they'd been expecting it all along. They probably had.

When Stan took his first step across, I held my breath. His hooves clacked on the metal below, and I gripped the reins tightly. The bridge had no railings and was only about five feet wide. Given that it spanned over a hundred feet, it *had* to be structurally unsound. No engineer would approve it.

But it'd been made by magic.

Still, that didn't keep me from squeezing my eyes closed to keep from looking down at the gorge below.

You're doing great!

Muffin's voice sounded from behind me. I peeked back over my shoulder and spotted the three cats sitting on the other side of the bridge, apparently unwilling to cross until we'd cleared it.

I scowled at them.

What? Muffin meowed. *Just letting you test it. I'd like to hang on to my nine lives, thank you very much. But really, you're doing fabulous!*

Given that he'd pulled the same trick with the beanstalk in the fairytale realm, I had to figure that my cat was just as afraid of heights as I was.

"Jerk!" I called, but couldn't help my grin.

He made some kind of strange wheezing sound that I took to be a laugh.

By the time I turned back around, Stan was stepping off the bridge onto the other side. My muscles turned to jelly as the adrenaline faded.

"Give me demons any day." I maneuvered my mount to join Lachlan, who was ahead of me by about a dozen feet.

"Which way?" he asked.

I studied the terrain ahead of us. More field, as before, but there was a dark speck in the distance. A forest? I pointed toward it. "That way."

Lachlan nodded and gave his horse a nudge. She picked up the pace and my horse followed suit.

As we neared the spot that I'd spied earlier, I realized it wasn't a forest. "It's giant hedges." I squinted at them, noticing a dark gap right in the middle. "With an entrance. The black stain cuts right through it."

Muffin appeared at my side, galloping along to keep up with Stan. *It's a maze shaped like a Celtic knot.*

I looked down at him. "How do you know that?"

He shot me an incredulous look. *Cat Sìth, remember? These are my stomping grounds.*

"Do you know the way through the maze?"

I haven't stomped that way before. He disappeared, as if he didn't want to hear my laughter.

We slowed our mounts as we neared the hedges. Stan went right through the entrance of the maze, confident as you please, then stopped dead.

I sighed. Too good to be true that my horse would know the way. And the black stain cut right through the maze, going into the hedges. It hadn't burned the wall of foliage away, though, so if we wanted to make it through, we had to do it the old-fashioned way.

There were four options for our forward progress, and my druid sense didn't immediately ignite.

I closed my eyes and sucked in a deep breath, calling upon my magic from deep within me. It glowed faintly. I used Lachlan's trick of thinking about *why* I needed this magic.

It flared to life within me, bright and strong. I gripped the reins to steady myself and called it forward. Power swelled within my chest, ready to break free.

My arms began to burn, the tattoos dampening my magic.

I winced. *Fates, this sucked.*

But I got a faint idea of which way to go. The same vague sense that I'd gotten before we'd entered the maze. It pulled left. I turned toward the two paths on the left, catching sight of two spectral white wolves standing at the end of one path.

They were as tall as my waist when I was standing, each with a shaggy coat and glowing eyes.

Muffin appeared next to me, hissing. *The Cŵn Annwn.*

"What are they?" My magic—what little I could feel of it, with the tattoo interfering—tugged me toward them.

The spectral hours of Annwn, the Welch Celtic Otherworld.

"I'm going to follow them."

Muffin hissed again but didn't disagree.

"This way." I nudged Stan so that he'd follow the hounds. Lachlan's horse fell into step behind me, and we started deeper into the maze. The walls rose tall on either side of us, soaring thirty feet overhead. The foliage was thick and green, creating an impenetrable wall. Even the sun was blocked from in here, making it increasingly difficult to navigate.

The hounds led us through the maze, racing ahead on swift paws. Occasionally, I'd spot the stain on the ground as it cut through the maze. As long as I occasionally saw that, I knew we were going the right way.

When we entered a clearing, Stan halted. I nearly flew over

his head, saving myself at the last minute by tightening my legs around him and gripping the saddle's pommel.

In the middle of the clearing, a woman sat at a well. She wore a long green dress embroidered with golden thread. The same thread had been woven through her red hair, making it glint like gold. Her magic rolled toward me, strong and fierce. It poked inside my mind. I winced, trying to shut off my thoughts.

Lachlan stopped next to me, his horse pawing the ground apprehensively.

The woman looked up, her blue eyes shining in the low light of the clearing. "Ah, Warrior Druid. Here at last."

I nudged Stan, and he approached with a slow gait.

I looked between her and the well upon which she sat. It was a simple stone affair, but the water within beckoned to me. I could just imagine it, fresh and pure.

"I'm Ana Blackwood." I inclined my head.

"I am Cebhfhionn, and I preside over the Well of Knowledge."

That's why the well called to me so much. I dragged my gaze from it and looked at her. "You're a goddess."

"One of many. My gifts are healing, knowledge, and a bit of power over the mind."

Would I get any of those? I didn't know how to politely ask if she was one of the goddesses who would donate a bit of her magic to me. As I understood it from Bree, some Norse gods had agreed to give her a bit of their gifts, and others hadn't.

I decided to just spit it out. "I'm trying to pass through the maze to get to the sacred grove. Do you have any advice?"

"Straight to the point, then." She smiled. "You are our chosen one, Ana. But are you worthy of it?"

Oh fates, the million-dollar question. "I'm trying to be."

"Not a bad answer. I'm sure that you can see that I cherish intelligence and cleverness."

I nodded.

"A riddle, then. And you may drink from the Well of Knowledge. Just a sip. Just enough to help you find your way from this place."

Oh, hell. Riddles.

"Which rock is as light as a feather?" she asked.

I frowned, my mind spinning. Pumice was a lightweight rock, wasn't it? But it still wasn't light as a feather. That would have to be something thin and tiny. A small amount of any rock?

No, she'd never take that. She hadn't said *how much* rock is as light as a feather.

I stared at the ground, my gaze catching on the clovers that littered the grass. Understanding pierced me. My head popped up. "A shamrock!"

She smiled and nodded. "Well done."

The *Cŵn Annwn* hounds circled the clearing, their eyes on me. Anxious energy seemed to vibrate from them. They didn't like the goddess. Somehow, I was sure of it.

Cebhfhionn gestured me closer. "Come, I'll give you a drink from the well."

I dismounted and approached. Had it really been this easy?

Muffin appeared next to the goddess, hissing at her. He arched his back and glared.

"Muffin! Be polite!"

Don't be a moron.

I frowned, slowing my approach. Up close, the well seemed to shimmer slightly. I blinked, and it looked solid and normal again.

Cebhfhionn gestured for me to come near, her gaze dropping to the sleeve of my jacket. "You have a stain there. Give it here and I'll wash it."

Muffin hissed again. *I don't like this. All is not as it seems.*

The well seemed to shimmer. I blinked.

Something was wrong. That riddle had been so easy. And what was up with the well?

"Give it here!" Cebhfhionn made a grabby hand gesture that looked a bit too aggressive for helping me with my clothes.

Back up, moron.

I did as Muffin commanded, walking backward toward Stan.

"Don't you want your drink from the well?" Cebhfhionn asked. "And your jacket needs tending to."

"Um, no thanks." Alarm bells were going off in my head like mad.

Cebhfhionn rose, her brow creased.

I jumped onto Stan's back as the air around her began to shimmer. She shifted from a red-haired woman into an old crone. The well disappeared, leaving a stream in its place.

The Bean Nighe! Muffin arched his back and hissed.

"The Bean Nighe," Lachlan said, as if he'd heard the cat, though he couldn't have. He nudged his mount into a trot. "Come on."

The hair on my arms stood on end as the old woman glared at me with dark eyes. "You'll regret this!"

"I don't know what *this* is, but I'm not regretting it." I directed my horse around her, and Stan jumped over the stream with ease.

Muffin joined me, trotting at my side. *She washes the clothes of those about to die.*

I turned back to look at the woman. "You were trying to kill me by washing my clothes?"

Hatred puckered her face as she stared at me.

"I'll take that as a yes."

"Dullahan!" she shrieked. "Come forth!"

Muffin hissed. *Oh crap!*

"What is it?" I demanded.

Run! Go horse, go! Muffin shrieked at Stan, who picked up speed.

I clung to him, hanging on for dear life. Lachlan's horse began to gallop, racing through the maze. The spectral hounds kept pace ahead of us, sprinting as fast as their long legs could carry them. Even they seemed frightened.

A galloping sounded from behind us, a horse's hooves kicking up the ground.

I turned to catch sight of it.

A shadowy, headless man pursued us, riding an enormous black horse. The figure carried his head in his hands. A grin stretched across his face, going from ear to ear.

A chill raced down my spine.

This creature was what the Bean Nighe had called for when she'd shrieked "Dullahan".

The Dullahan leaned forward on its mount and spurred it on, charging after us.

Go! Muffin meowed. *You can't defeat the Dullahan. He just needs to touch you to kill. There's no fighting back.*

Oh, hell.

My heart thundered as Stan galloped away from the Dullahan, sprinting through the maze. I bounced like I was riding a mechanical bull, barely managing to hold on.

Ahead of me, Lachlan rode like a freaking equestrian. As if he'd been born in a saddle. Stan followed the Cŵn Annwn, turning left and right and looping back around the curves of the knot.

Around me, the hedges began to shift, magic swelling. Faces appeared, but we went so fast that I could hardly make out details.

"Get to the water," they whispered. Branches pointed like arms.

Stan neighed, charging onward.

We burst from the maze, out into an open field. Stan bucked, then darted forward so fast that I lost my seat, tumbling off. A curse sounded from up ahead as I slammed into the ground, pain shooting through me.

Lachlan had fallen off, too.

The horses had ditched us.

4

They'd taken us as far as they could, and now they were getting the heck out of Dodge, the Dullahan scaring them off.

I scrambled to my feet and whirled around.

The Dullahan burst out of the hedges, headed straight for us. The Cats of Catastrophe chased him, heads low and strides determined. Princess Snowflake III leapt, her white fur whipping in the wind, and landed on the horse's haunches, digging in with her claws.

The horse neighed and bucked, buying us precious seconds.

I turned back to Lachlan, who'd already shifted into his black lion form. His black fur glinted in the sunlight, and he roared.

The message was clear. I sprinted toward him, then leaped onto his back and clung tightly to his mane. He took off, racing across the grass, away from the Dullahan.

My heart thundered, deafening, and I crouched low, the wind whipping at my hair, as Lachlan charged away. In the distance, a river snaked through the field.

Get to the water. That was what the spirits in the hedges had said.

Lachlan raced for the river, leaping over rocks and shrubs. The Cats of Catastrophe joined us, sprinting alongside.

"We need to cross!" I screamed.

He veered for the thinnest part of the river, crouching low and leaping over in one smooth glide. He landed on the other side with a hard thud. The cats followed, jumping unnaturally far. I turned, heart in my throat.

The Dullahan had skidded to a stop, a grimace stretched across the head that he carried in his arms. Magic swirled in the river, sparkling and bright.

A massive black stallion leapt out of the glittering water. The horse charged the Dullahan, whose own mount gave a terrified shriek and whirled on its hind legs, spinning and racing back toward the maze.

The black stallion gave chase, galloping after the Dullahan.

Panting, I sagged on Lachlan's back. "What the heck was that?"

Muffin meowed. *Kelpie. A water spirit.*

"And the natural enemy of the Dullahan, it seems." I climbed off Lachlan's back.

He shifted back to human and scrubbed his hand over his face. "To be honest, I wasn't sure I'd get us out of that."

My heart was still slowing from the adrenaline. My muscles felt like pudding. Without him, I wouldn't have stood a chance at outrunning the Dullahan. "But you did. Thanks."

The sound of galloping hooves sounded from behind, and I turned, heart leaping into my throat.

The Kelpie cantered toward us, his black coat gleaming in the light. He slowed as he neared. A sparkling green light swirled around him, and he shifted into the form of a young man with dark eyes. His long hair was threaded with water weeds, and he was as pale as a lifelong IT specialist.

Princess Snowflake III sauntered up to him, inspecting him. Bojangles followed, along with Muffin.

Did he smell like fish?

I sniffed subtly, but only got a whiff of the scent of a fresh river.

"Thank you for driving off the Dullahan," Lachlan said.

"Is there anything we can do for you?" I asked. It was good form to return kindness with kindness, after all. And I could use all the allies I could get in this crazy realm.

The Kelpie inspected us. Well, me, mostly. His gaze traveled over me as if I were a workhorse he was thinking of buying. Then he nodded, seeming to have made up his mind.

"You must stop the invaders," he said. "The old tales say that one such as you will stop a force that poisons Otherworld. Do this, and I am repaid."

"There are tales about me?"

"Aye, if you are who I think you are. But you must succeed. Otherworld depends on you."

"Who is invading?" I pointed to the black scar on the land that we were following. It had come out of the maze along with us.

"I didn't see them. I was underwater and the Dullahan approved of their presence, so he didn't gallop after them and wake me. But I felt something, even underneath my river. A darkness. You'll have to be strong and cunning to defeat them, for they possess immense strength."

I nodded. "I'll do it."

"Go, then. And if you meet the fae, do not partake of the food in their realm or you may never escape." With that, he turned and walked off.

The cats looked at him longingly but didn't chase after.

My druid sense pulled me away from the river, so I turned and set off. Lachlan joined me, and we walked in silence. Thoughts raced through my mind. Who was invading Otherworld? What did they want?

Muffin meowed. *Are we there yet?*

I glanced down at him. "I have no idea, but you sound like a kid in the back of a minivan."

I wouldn't turn down a Happy Meal.

"Or a bite of the Kelpie?"

He looked tasty. Yummy fishy horse man. He started to purr. *But really, how far are we?*

"I don't know. My druid sense is pulling me along, but it's vague." I rubbed my arms, disliking the new tattoos. The premonition magic had already been wonky, but these made it even harder to use.

Fortunately, I liked a challenge.

As long as it didn't kill me.

And Otherworld seemed determined to kill me.

We walked for over an hour before the terrain changed, going from rolling green field to forest. Oak trees loomed around us, shading us from the midday sun. The black scar on the land cut through the forest, forming a path that we followed.

We were about a quarter mile into the forest when Lachlan grabbed my arm. I stopped abruptly.

Lachlan pointed ahead.

I squinted through the forest, barely catching sight of a flash of white. I leaned left to peer around some trees and spotted it. "There are ruins there."

"Aye."

We crept forward on silent feet, alert and wary. The black streak that scarred the land cut straight toward the white marble ruins. If our target had stopped here, it would be a great place from which to launch an attack. There was plenty of cover.

I drew a dagger from the ether. Even the cats slunk along, their backs low to the ground as they prowled.

As we neared, I caught the smell of water. The white structure was larger than I expected, and they weren't ruins at all. The white marble pillars had made me *think* they were, since that was how places like this normally appeared on earth.

But it was in great shape.

The pillars and low walls surrounded a central pool that was filled with milky blue water. The stain crept into the pool, dyeing part of it black. Heavy magic hung on the air, something powerful and dangerous. It made my skin crawl and heart race.

Lachlan and I ducked behind a tree and peered at the pillars that could hide enemies. The cats crouched next to us, ready to pounce.

"Those are baths," I whispered. "Like the Roman baths, or the one at Pompeii. But they're *here*."

"It can't be a coincidence," Lachlan said.

"No, it can't. The Celts and the Romans had been linked for centuries. Two great cultures at war." The quick search I'd done on the Celts hadn't provided much research, but a few sources had made a big deal about the Romans. "Their religions even mixed in some areas. After years of living together and fighting, they shared aspects of culture. Especially in England."

"Like the Roman baths in Bath," Lachlan said.

"Exactly."

I shivered. So, this probably wasn't a coincidence, but I wasn't sure exactly what it meant.

A light flashed, golden and bright, and a figure appeared by the pool. She wore long white robes and glowed like a beacon.

There was something familiar about her. Like I'd seen her before. I didn't recognize her serene features, but her magic...

Fates.

She was the goddess who'd appeared in the stone circle in the fairytale realm, and again in my dream.

Except I'd thought she'd been a dude?

Her magic though...

I stepped out from behind the pillar. Lachlan reached for my arm, but I evaded him.

"It's okay," I murmured.

"Ana Blackwood. The Warrior Druid." The goddess's voice rumbled with power, deep and sure.

Yep, same one as before. Her voice had thrown me off.

"Sulis?" I asked.

"Indeed. I was the one who gave you the gift of light. Of life."

"That's what my glowing white magic is? The light of life?"

"In a sense, yes. It is light in its purest, most healing form. It can drive away sickness and darkness, and even control some plants and animal life."

Wow. I rubbed my arms as I continued to approach her. "I'm having trouble with it, though."

She nodded toward my arms, her golden hair gleaming in the light. "Your tattoos, I presume?"

"Exactly."

"They are the mark of The Druid. Part of the transitional process. They will help you master and control your magic, as long as you can unite their power with your life force."

"How the heck do I do that?" I stopped at the edge of the marble platform upon which she stood. The pool behind her gleamed with a pale light. The black splotch from the dark magic that streaked across the land looked like an oil slick.

"The torc that you seek in the sacred grove will help."

"I'm seeking a torc in the sacred grove? What is that?"

"It is a sacred piece of jewelry. A talisman, of sorts, that is worn around the neck. You won't be able to meet all of the gods who give you powers, so they won't be there in person to help you learn their magic. Like I am. But the torc will help you understand and use their magic."

I kept stealing glances at the water behind her, unable to help myself. The evil that had left this stain made worry churn in my gut. I couldn't keep my eyes off it. "What happened here? Did you see who passed?"

"They were shadows of darkness that submerged themselves in the bath, partaking of the healing waters. They grew stronger, then continued on their way."

Crap. Stronger was not good.

"I do not know who they were, but they felt familiar, somehow." A scowl crossed her serene features. "They clearly felt entitled to my baths, yet they did not leave an offering."

I didn't want to point out that it wasn't really the style of invaders to respect local customs.

Sulis caught my eye. "Together, we will drive this darkness from the baths. It will help you learn to control your magic."

Heck yeah. This sounded promising.

Sulis gestured me forward. I glanced back at Lachlan, who waited at the side, alert and wary.

I stepped toward Sulis, who reached out and laid her fingertips against my arm. I jerked as if a live wire had hit me. Her touch was electric and strong, though not bad. It felt like pure power streaking through me, reaching deep into my middle and pulling on the light power that had been so hard to control. It flared bright, filling me up.

My arms burned, but I ignored it.

"Direct your light at the pool," Sulis said.

I did as she commanded, envisioning my light shining on the dark water. It surged from me, easier and faster than it ever had. Lachlan's help had opened the floodgates, but this was the water pouring forth.

It shot straight into the heart of the darkness, blasting it away. Within seconds, the water gleamed pure and bright. A sense of calm fell over the baths, making them feel like the most relaxing place I'd ever been to. Birds began to sing, and flower blooms fell from the trees.

The black scar in the earth still existed on either side of the marble and pool of water, but we'd fixed the bath itself.

I struggled to catch my breath, trying not to pant like a dog after a long run on the beach. That had taken a lot out of me. I couldn't defeat all of the darkness in Otherworld—not when it took so much magic to do this little bit—but I was thrilled to have fixed the bath.

"*That* is what the torc will do for you," Sulis said. "It is a direct conduit with the gods who have given you their power. The magic of The Druid is a difficult thing. Wild and untamed. You need our help to control it, and long ago, we imbued the sacred torc with the magic to help you master the powers we will give you."

"So you mean it's not entirely my fault that I haven't gotten a handle on my magic?"

"You've done better than anyone would have expected." Her gaze moved to Lachlan. "In large part because of your friend. His guidance allowed you some control. But you will progress no farther without the torc. It's the other half of the druid magic, a sacred item that is required for you to complete your transition."

I nodded, simultaneously confused and relieved. I'd hated feeling like such a half-assed Magica who couldn't get a grip on her magic. Knowing that there was a reason why...

It was awesome.

And I was going to do whatever it took to get ahold of that torc.

"Thank you, Sulis."

She let go of my arm and stepped back. The sense of control

that I'd had vanished, like a flaming match had died inside of me.

Oh, heck yeah, I was going to hunt down that torc. Clearly, I needed it.

"Be careful on your journey," Sulis said. "You will meet the fae in their realm. Respect their customs and they will respect you. But if you do not, you will spend a thousand years with them."

Yeah, I didn't want to do that. "Where will I meet them?"

"It will be quite obvious. Your gift of premonition will guide you. And remember. Before you confront the evil that is invading this realm, you must get the torc. It is everything."

I nodded. The puzzle pieces were really starting to come together. "Thank you."

She disappeared on a flash of light. I turned to Lachlan. "Ready to go find this torc?"

"Aye."

I grinned. We set off, departing the baths. We were only about a dozen feet away when a splash sounded. I glanced back. The Cats of Catastrophe had leapt into the baths. Princess Snowflake III and Bojangles each looked like a drowned rat. Muffin looked as skinny as usual, so that was no change.

Muffin meowed. *Get in! The water's great!*

The cats seemed to glow with the light of health. I stopped walking. Sulis had said that the evil had grown stronger once it had gone into the bath.

"Hang on, Lachlan. I want to try something." I returned to the bath and knelt at the edge. My muscles were weak and my insides felt empty from using my magic with Sulis. I dipped my fingertips in the water.

Strength and health flowed through me like a golden light. I gasped as it filled me, making my head spin. The magical energy that I'd used was replenished. Even my body felt better, like I'd had a good meal and a nap.

Lachlan joined me.

"Try it," I said.

He dipped his fingertips in the water, a low gasp escaping his lips. He even looked healthier and stronger, which was saying something, considering he normally looked like he crushed semitrucks and ate them for breakfast.

He looked at me, his dark eyes turning heavy. "The evil that invaded this place bathed here. They took this power into themselves."

Oh, fates. He had a point. This was like a magical battery charger, and it had just made our enemy a lot stronger.

5

After leaving a tribute at the baths—I left a dagger from my collection and Lachlan left a small vial of healing potion —we continued on our way. We didn't have to walk far before the forest gave way to more rolling fields. The Cats of Catastrophe had refused to leave the baths, mostly because Muffin had fashioned a raft out of twigs and leaves and was lounging like he was waiting for someone to bring him a piña colada.

I assumed they would show up eventually, though. It seemed to be their style.

The black scar in the earth cut through the land, headed straight for a large hill before veering right. My druid sense continued to drag me along toward the sacred grove, slightly stronger now that I'd dipped my fingers in Sulis's healing bath. It always pulled in the direction of the black scar, indicating that the invaders and me were on the same track toward the sacred grove.

As we neared the place where the scar deviated away from the hill, my druid sense pulled me toward the hill.

"That's weird," I muttered.

"What is?" Lachlan asked.

I pointed toward the scar. "My premonition gift wants me to deviate and go toward the hill."

The ground beneath us trembled, cutting off my words. Light glowed through the grass. I glanced down. A swirling design formed beneath my feet, three spirals attached together at the middle.

Lachlan wasn't even looking at it.

"Don't you see that?" I asked.

"See what? I'm looking at the dogs."

I glanced up, catching sight of the two spectral white hounds who had guided us through the maze. They stood near the hill, watching us with silent majesty.

I looked back down at the light under my feet. "You don't see the light in the ground? It's a swirl."

He squinted at the grass, clearly confused. "I see grass."

"So, just me, then." What the heck was it?

"Aye, appears so."

The hill in front of us began to glow as well, a door appearing in the side. "Do you see *that*?"

"Aye. A door."

It opened, and two figures stepped out. They wore sweeping green dresses, and their eyes glowed with power. Pointed ears peaked through their hair, and their figures were slender and willowy. The hounds strolled up to stand next to them.

"The fae." I studied them as they approached, debating.

I needed to follow the scar in the earth, but my druid sense dragged me toward the fae. The druids and my mother had made it clear that I had to get the torc before I confronted the invaders. Perhaps this was part of that.

"We have to speak to them," I said. "I feel it."

"I doubt they're going to let us off the hook, anyway." Lachlan nodded toward the weapons on their backs. One carried a bow and the other a sword. Despite their dresses and slender forms, they were clearly battle fae.

The fae on the left spoke, her blond hair gleaming in the light. "Warrior Druid?"

I nodded. "I think that's me."

"I am Errawen." She gestured to her partner, a dark-haired fae. "This is Bren. We are here to guide you to Annwn."

Of course. The white hounds were the hounds of Annwn. They'd led us here.

"I've heard that not many people are invited there," Lachlan said. "Yet you invite us?"

"We saw you help Sulis," Errawen said. "Which means you must be good."

"You know Sulis?" I studied them. They were beautiful, but danger vibrated from them.

"We do. We are from different branches of the Celtic pantheon. She is Romano Celtic, a melding of British and Roman belief, while we are Irish. But we know her."

This pantheon really was huge, stretching all the way across Europe.

"What will we find in Annwn?" I asked.

"Answers, I believe," Bren said.

I could definitely use some answers, so I nodded. We followed them toward the door to Annwn. As soon as I stepped through, magic took my breath away. It felt unlike anything I'd ever experienced. As if I'd stepped into a whole new world in which the very air was made of different stuff. Magic, mostly.

We followed them deep into the earth, taking a winding path that led downward. The space widened up until it felt like we weren't underground at all. A pale sun even shone overhead.

"How does this work?" I asked.

"Another realm," Bren said. "Everything is not always as it

seems. We live under the hill, but not underground like rabbits in a warren."

"Certainly not," Errawen said.

We walked through a forest of trees with pale trunks. They were almost a silvery tan. The leaves themselves looked to be pure silver, and lights glittered through the branches.

Fairy lights. Just like at the enchanted grove back at the Protectorate. The forest gave way to a village filled with beautiful pale wooden houses. They were carved with delicate scrollwork, and the roofs were made of pale gray tile. Fae faces peered out at us through the windows.

"Have you experienced any trouble from the evil that is making its way through Otherworld?" I asked.

"We have someone who would like to talk to you about that," Errawen said.

Well, that was clear.

She led us across a delicate bridge that arched over a glittering river. It sparkled with blue light deep within, and I was simultaneously drawn to and repelled by it.

"We're nearly there." Bren led us toward a tall palace built of pale wood with silver trim. It was almost too beautiful to be real. The large courtyard housed a sparkling silver fountain that burbled with water. Desperately, I wanted to drink from the fountain, but I remembered what the Kelpie had said. We must not eat or drink anything from this realm if we ever wanted to leave.

And I did want to leave.

As beautiful as it was, something in the air here made me uncomfortable.

Fortunately, Lachlan still had the pack of food from my mother.

"Odd place, isn't it?" Lachlan whispered.

"Yeah." Like the fae themselves. Beautiful but dangerous.

Offputtingly so. I wouldn't put it past them to try to coax us to eat food and stay forever.

Except, maybe they didn't even want us. I'd make a terrible guest.

Fortunately, they led us around the side of the castle. I didn't want to go in the castle, no matter how beautiful it promised to be.

At the side of the castle, there was a small grove of trees. Silver birches, tall and slender. In the middle of the grove sat a well, guarded over by a woman.

I gasped. "Cebhfhionn."

She turned to us, her pale eyes bright. "The real one, this time."

I believed her. I might not trust the elves, but this was the real Cebhfhionn, unlike the Bean Nighe back at the maze. The Bean Nighe had possessed a powerful magic, but it had been nothing like Cebhfhionn's.

Her magic vibrated, strong and bright. Like Sulis's magic, it was so powerful that it nearly knocked me off my feet. There was no doubt that this was the true goddess.

I approached, stopping about ten feet from her. She wore a brilliant white dress shot through with golden thread that matched her hair. "So you know you have an imposter?"

"She's still in the maze?" Cebhfhionn asked.

I nodded.

"Aye, that doesn't surprise me. The Bean Nighe will transform into whatever she thinks you want. The maze helps her."

"What did I want?" I asked. "Why did she pretend to be you?"

"I would think it's obvious. You want knowledge, and I represent that."

"Okay, you have a point." I'd thought I wanted many things

—my sisters' safety, to earn my place at the Protectorate, to master my magic.

But at the heart of it, I wanted knowledge. In the end, knowledge would get me everything I wanted.

"Why did you call me here?" I asked. "I'm meant to follow the path to the sacred grove. It should align with the path taken by the evil that has invaded Otherworld."

"Aye, that is your mission. But first, I wanted to offer you some water from the well of knowledge." She dipped her silver bucket into the well and drew out some water.

"Why?" I asked.

"You are the Druid Dragon God, and this is my gift to you. Like Sulis gave you her light and the druids gave you their sense of premonition, I'd like to give you the gift of knowledge. It will help you control your magic, and it will sharpen your sense of premonition."

"Thank you." I stepped forward, eager for anything that would help me. Then I pulled up short. "Wait, I'm not supposed to eat or drink anything here."

She smiled. "Ah, smart, Ana. This is true. Someone has warned you about the dangers of the fae realm."

"The Kelpie."

"He is a smart one." She smiled. "But fear not. You will not drink this water. You must bathe your hands and face in it."

"I've been having a lot of magical baths today."

She gave me a quizzical look, then her brow smoothed. "Ah, Sulis and her baths."

"Exactly."

"That didn't hurt you, and neither will this. As long as you don't drink it. Humans—even magical ones—cannot handle the full strength of the water within my well. It is why I must guard it from them, here at this underground palace. But you are strong enough to bathe in its waters."

I nodded, liking the compromise. I wanted the knowledge and the power that she promised. And if this kept me from the long-lasting side effects of spending eternity in Annwn, I'd take it.

But I couldn't stop myself from sparing one last glance for Lachlan. He looked torn, but finally, he nodded, as if agreeing that this was a good idea.

I'd have done it even without his approval, but I felt a bit better since he'd deemed it safe.

I stopped in front of Cebhfhionn, and she held out the bucket. Carefully, I rinsed my hands within. Then my face.

My mind seemed to clear, clarity of thought falling over me and making me gasp.

My druid sense tugged hard, as if it had been given a hit of an energy drink.

"I can see that it has worked," Cebhfhionn said. "But you must use it wisely, in pursuit of good."

"Speaking of that, do you know anything about the evil that is cutting through Otherworld and leaving a dark stain on the earth?"

She nodded. "The evil bypassed our realm, of course. It was not welcome here. But my scouts report that the evil consisted of three shadowy figures who are nearly opaque. Women, they thought, but they could not be sure."

A lightning bolt of recognition shot through me. My eyes flared wide, and I glanced back at Lachlan. His face betrayed almost nothing, as usual, but even his eyes were slightly wide. He met my gaze and nodded.

He agreed.

The three figures could be the same that we'd encountered a few days ago—the ones in the cloaks. The cloaked figures had been Lachlan's nemeses ever since they'd stolen the *ancientus* spell.

They'd become mine, too.

I turned back to Cebhfhionn. "Were they powerful?"

"Very. When our guards confronted them, they used their magic to blast them backward. Like a sonic boom, but more powerful."

I rubbed my stomach, remembering the pain of being hit with that type of blow.

"Yet they didn't come here," I said.

"No. But we have a vested interest in stopping them. They may not be coming after us now, but they are hurting our fellow citizens here in Otherworld. We may be a loose collection of cultures and individual religions, but it is still our duty to watch out for one another." She shrugged. "Anyway, they may grow tired of destroying the rest of Otherworld and come here for us eventually."

She had a point. "So you don't know what they are after?"

"I do not. Only that their strength is growing and they don't hesitate to kill."

"We'll stop them," I said. "We have to."

"That is true. Your destiny is linked with theirs, this I know. This is a battle you were meant to fight, Ana. Perhaps *the* battle."

Suddenly, exhaustion pulled at me. Almost as if the strength of Sulis's bath had worn off and the difficulty of the day was catching up with me. I could still feel her power within me, but I needed to recharge.

"You must rest." Her gaze traveled behind me to Lachlan. "You must, as well. When you encounter the evil, you must be strong and able to fight."

She had a point there. But... "We can't stop. We need to catch them before they get whatever they are after."

"Even they must rest," she said. "And so, too, should you. Tomorrow morning, we'll give you fae horses that will carry you far faster than you'd ever make it on foot. They can't go out at night—their vision isn't good enough—but in the daylight, they'll take you. You won't lose any time, and you'll get some sleep."

I believed her. Maybe because I wanted to, but she had a vested interest in us stopping the invaders, so I doubted she'd lie to us.

I turned to Lachlan. He looked exhausted as well. He nodded.

I turned to Cebhfhionn. "We'll stay the night. Thank you."

They set us up in a cute little cottage on the main street. It was for guests, apparently, and the whole place was made of pale wood and silver paint. All of the cushions were white, and the place definitely felt like a fairy cottage.

I had a quick shower in the strangest little room I'd ever seen. It was lined with gray stone like a normal shower, but the water poured from flowers that grew out of the ceiling. It even smelled good.

By the time I was clean, my stomach was rumbling. I changed back into my clothes, which were only semi-dirty since they weren't coated in blood, and traded places with Lachlan.

While he showered, I dug into the backpack that the druids had given us. There had to be magic involved, because no matter how many things I removed from the bag, it never emptied.

Eventually, once I had a whole lot of stuff from every level of the food pyramid, plus a bottle of wine, I closed the bag. By the time Lachlan returned, I'd made a nice little platter of sliced meats and cheeses, along with some fresh veggies and fruit.

"That looks amazing," he said.

I did a half bow from my seat at the little table and grinned. "Thanks, made it myself."

He joined me, and we dug in.

"Wine, even?" He took a sip.

"You wouldn't believe that bag." Once we'd sated the worst of our hunger, I looked at him. "So, the three figures. I think they must be the three shadows that drifted out of the cloaked figure when I removed their cloak."

He swallowed and nodded. "Given that they have a type of sonic boom power as well, and a connection with Italy, I'd say you're right."

"But how the heck is this all related?"

He leaned back in his chair, expression thoughtful. "First, they were after the *ancientus* charm to bring back a spell from the past. Second, they went after the power source provided by Arach's heart."

"And now they are after strength and knowledge here. But for what?"

"Whatever their end goal is. Which is pretty damned unclear right now."

I bit into a bar of chocolate—had the Celts really had chocolate, or was this an import?—and mulled it over. "We need to figure something out at the sacred grove."

He nodded. "You're getting better with your magic, though."

"I am. I can feel it. This place is really helping. Each step on this journey has made me stronger. I just hope I can master the rest of my magic."

"I have faith in you."

"Thanks. I'm going to call my sisters, all right? I want to let them know what's up."

"Sure. I'll clean up."

I went to the other side of the room and pressed my fingers to my comms charm. "Bree? Rowan?"

"Yeah?" Rowan's voice crackled through the connection, as if she were farther away than normal. Probably because we

were in Otherworld, which wasn't truly on earth. "Are
you okay?"

"Fine. But we've found some info we want to pass along." I
relayed everything I'd learned to her.

"All right, thanks. I'll tell Jude. But be careful, Ana, okay?"

"Definitely. You, too."

"Love you."

"Love you back." I killed the connection and joined Lachlan
where he sat on what I assumed was a fae version of a couch. It
was like a large cushion made of soft white fabric. Sinking into it
was like sinking into a cloud. But the lack of support meant that
I drifted right into Lachlan's side.

As soon as my skin touched his, my breath caught.

This was the first time we'd been together alone and hadn't
been fighting for our lives. And the Cats of Catastrophe weren't
here. I couldn't imagine what that peanut gallery would have to
say if I kissed Lachlan in front of them.

I turned to look at him, trying not to show how affected I was
by his nearness. The last time we'd been really alone together,
we'd decided not to pretend that there wasn't something
between us.

But what did that *mean*? And where would it lead?

The questions made me so uncertain that I decided to go
with another question instead. One that had been bugging me
for a while.

"Why did you hesitate to admit that there was something
between us? You said the whole *we work together* thing was just
an excuse. What was the real reason?"

A sad look crossed his face, but it was distant. Like he was in
the past instead of here in the future with me. He wrapped a
strong arm around my shoulders. I leaned into him, waiting.

For a while, he didn't speak. I was about to bug him when he
finally opened his mouth.

"When I was young, I loved a girl."

"How young?"

"Seventeen."

"So it's been a while, old man?"

He chuckled, and I was glad to get the sound out of him. The air was almost too heavy otherwise.

"What happened with her?"

"We were walking in Edinburgh one night. In the Grassmarket. The bars had closed, and it was too late to be out. It was during the Difficulties."

"The Difficulties?"

"Aye. A period when law and order wasn't as easily maintained. There were more demons about then, wreaking havoc as you'd expect. The government instituted a curfew for anyone who didn't want to get in trouble with them, but we were young and stupid."

I'd never heard of the Difficulties, but then, I'd been struggling to survive in Death Valley at the time and hadn't had much —or any—knowledge of the outside world. "I have a hard time imagining you were ever stupid."

"When I was young? Yes. I was infatuated. Totally lost my mind. We shouldn't have been out, but we were. And we weren't paying attention. *I* wasn't paying attention. All I could see was her. Until the demons came."

"Oh no."

He nodded. "We fought back. I took out six, but there were ten. By the time help arrived, we were both nearly dead."

"Oh, Lachlan." I couldn't imagine how terrible that must have been. In pain. Afraid. Young. "What happened then?"

"Recovery was an ugly process. Our relationship didn't survive it."

"I'm sorry."

"That part, I'm not sorry about. We were never meant to be.

But her injuries..." He sounded agonized. "I couldn't bear it. If I hadn't been so infatuated, so obsessed, I would have been more on my guard. We wouldn't have been out at night. Or if we had been, we'd have stuck to the safer streets. I vowed I wouldn't let anything like that happen again."

"Which is why you made up the excuse that we couldn't be together."

"Exactly. I wasn't *quite* ready to bare my worst failing to you. But when I started to feel something for you—something I've never felt before, not even with her, I knew I was in trouble."

"I can take care of myself, you know." His story sliced at my heart. "But I don't need you to be watching out for me all the time. I've managed fine on my own since I was thirteen."

I felt him turn to look at me, so I met his gaze. Conviction burned within the dark depths of his eyes. "I know. And that's what changed. I realized that you *could* take care of yourself. Better than I can take care of myself, half the time."

"I wouldn't say that. I've seen you fight." But the words mollified me.

"I want to protect you, Ana. I can't help it. I *need* to. But I also want you. And I recognize that you're more than capable on your own. It was stupid of me."

I liked what he was saying. Liked it *a lot*. "Well, don't be stupid anymore. Kiss me."

A rakish grin swiped across his face right before he pulled me to him. His thick arms wrapped around my back, and I reveled in his strength.

I crushed my mouth against his, my breath already coming fast. He kissed like he couldn't get enough of me. Like I was oxygen to a dying man.

My head spun as his mouth moved over mine, strong and sure. He tasted like wine and something that was indescribably him. I ran my hands up and down his back, over his shoulders and chest. I couldn't get enough of him.

He growled low in his throat, an animal noise that lit my senses on fire. "I can't get enough of you, Ana."

"Same." I kissed my way down his neck, loving the taste of him. "I've never felt like this before."

"I'm damned certain I'll never feel like this again."

I moved my lips back to his, and he devoured me, so skilled that my head began to spin. As he lowered me back onto the couch, I was certain that I never wanted to kiss anyone else, ever again.

6

The next morning, after waking up with Lachlan on the fluffy cloud couch, we had a quick breakfast that involved far more smiles than any other breakfast I'd ever had. Last night, we'd kissed for over an hour—I wasn't ready for more—then fallen asleep in each other's arms.

It had been the best night of my life.

I was well and truly infatuated and trying my best to play it cool. I was probably failing, but in fairness, Lachlan was clearly not totally cool himself. I kept catching him looking at me with this goofy smile on his face. Considering that his brand of attractiveness was the slightly scary kind—all dark hair and sharp angles and wicked dark eyes—it was pretty awesome.

My ego was definitely a fan. And so was my heart.

After eating, we met Bren and Errawen, our fae guides. They led us back up the path toward the exit from Annwn. Each of them led a majestic white horse. The hounds followed us, silent sentinels who walked on soundless paws.

"Be careful," Errawen said as we stepped out into the dawn light. "Otherworld has never seen such a threat as this. The destruction that it is causing...." She looked toward the dark scar in the land, her eyes sad. "I've never seen anything like it."

"I'll fix it." I had no idea how, but I *would*. This was my second home, in a strange way. I couldn't leave it like this.

"Stay alert," Errawen said. "Take help when it appears. Otherworld wants you to succeed in this. It will help you. You aren't terribly far from the sacred grove now, but you must be prepared to make a sacrifice."

"I will be." Yikes. Sacrifice never sounded fun. "And thank you."

They nodded once, then handed us the reins. "The horses will help you go fast. When you're done, release them. They will find their way home."

"Thank you." I patted my horse on the neck, noticing that her white fur sparkled slightly. Her mane was a pale blue, along with her hooves. She looked a lot like what I'd imagine a unicorn would look like, though she had no horn. As a kid, I would have lost my mind over this fae pony. Adult me was having a bit of a fit as well, honestly.

Bren and Errawen turned and went back into the hill. The door disappeared.

Lachlan and I mounted our horses. We hadn't seen hide nor hair of the cats, though I had a feeling Muffin would like to ride on this horse.

I didn't need to tell the horse to set off. She picked up the pace and went straight toward the black scar on the earth, following the premonition that dragged me in that direction. It was almost as if she were connected to me, knowing which way I wanted to go. Lachlan's mount kept pace with mine, and we galloped across the fields, making excellent time toward the sacred grove.

When a pond glittered in the distance, I pointed. "See that?"

"Aye. We headed that way?"

"Yep."

My horse went faster, slowing only once we had reached the pond. It was about a hundred yards wide. The air on the other side shimmered as if something there was hidden by magic.

I dismounted and patted the horse's neck. "Thank you."

She whinnied and began to chomp grass, going straight for the clover. Every one she plucked up had four leaves. The luckiest horse on the planet. Or in Otherworld, at least.

Lachlan jumped off his mount, who began to mow the lawn as well, cleaning out every clover in the place. I left them to it, following the black scar in the land as it stretched toward the pond.

Just like at Sulis's Roman baths, the water looked like it had an oil slick snaking through it.

"They've been here." I stepped up to the slick and bent over, peering at it. The stench of rotten meat wafted toward me, and I gagged, stumbling backward. "Wow, they're foul."

"Aye, that's the truth." Lachlan walked around the edge of the pond, peering into the depths. "There are weapons in the water."

"Weapons?" I joined him and spotted several old daggers and a sword. There was a shield, too, along with a small metal figurine. Understanding dawned. "They must be sacrifices. Remember what the fae said?"

"Aye. Which means that this must be something we have to decipher. Or do."

"Maybe we make a sacrifice?"

"Maybe."

I turned and inspected the land around us. About ten yards farther down the lakeshore, there was a large flat rock. It was shaped like a disc and set perfectly into the ground. I walked toward it, noticing that there were four indents carved into the rock. One in the center, and three around the edges, forming a triangle.

I climbed onto the rock and peered at one. It was shaped like a short sword, roughly two feet long with a slender hilt. The second one was a figurine, and the third a shield. In the middle, there was one shaped like a dagger. I looked between the lake and the platform, then at the hazy air across the pond. It was shaped roughly like a tree.

"Hey, Lachlan? Will you walk around the pond toward the tree? I want to test something."

"Aye." He started around the pond, going clockwise. I went counter-clockwise.

After about fifty yards, I slammed into an invisible barrier, just barely managing to stop before smashing my face.

"Yep. As I thought." I looked at Lachlan just in time to see him hit another barrier.

"I can't get through. There's a spell."

"I think I know what it is." I approached Lachlan, who met me at the flat stone disk. "There's a spell protecting whatever is on the other side of the lake, and we need to earn our way in. I think we have to find sacrifices in the lake that match the shape of the indentions on the stone." I pointed to the sword-shaped one. "That's what the fae meant about sacrifice."

Lachlan grinned. "Aye, you're onto something."

I turned toward the lake. "Our target already completed the task." The black oil snaked through the water, making me shudder. No way I was getting in that water as long as it was there. "I'm going to try to clean up the pond first."

"Good plan." He held out his palm. "Want a hand?"

"Sure." I smiled. Teamwork. I liked that. When I had the torc, it'd be easier to do this on my own. But for now, I'd take all the help I could get.

I gripped his hand, my body lighting up at his touch.

When his magic flowed into me, strength followed. I called upon my gift of light, catching onto it quickly. Sulis's help had broken a barrier inside of me, making it easier to call upon the gift.

The light barreled out of me, shooting straight toward the black oil and lighting it up. It disappeared instantly, leaving the lake clear and calm.

I grinned and let go of Lachlan's hand. "I like getting the hang of this."

"You're good at it." Lachlan stripped off his shirt, getting ready to go hunting for the appropriate sacrifices.

It wasn't easy not to stare, so I focused on taking off my boots. Next came my jacket, and since I didn't want to run around in wet clothes all day, I stripped off my jeans and shirt as well.

"Would it be rude to stare?" A bit of heat echoed in Lachlan's voice.

I shivered. "Frankly, I can't take the distraction. So eyes on your own paper."

He chuckled. "Agreed. But I *will* be thinking about you. Can't help that."

I grinned. "I'm fine with that."

He finished stripping down to his underwear, and we waded into the cool water.

I took one deep breath and submerged myself, opening my eyes underwater. Things were a bit distorted, but it was clear enough that I could make out the various weapons and other items scattered across the sand below.

My lungs burned as I tried to stay under as long as possible. When I spotted a sword about two feet long with the distinctive handle, I kicked hard toward it, cutting through the water.

It gleamed, calling to me, and I reached for it. I almost had it when a snake darted out from behind a rock. The beast was as thick as my thigh and as long as I was, a brilliant green thing with big yellow eyes.

I kicked away from it, shooting for the surface, but the water made me slow. Panic stabbed me as the snake wrapped around my legs. Briefly, I broke the surface and gasped, sucking in a ragged breath before the snake dragged me back down.

Water rushed around me. I bent over, calling my dagger from the ether and stabbing for the snake. He'd wrapped himself around my legs and was pulling me back to the bottom.

My blade plunged into his side. He didn't even flinch, just yanked me deeper. Fear screamed through me as I thrashed, trying to break free while stabbing at the serpent.

He's just too strong.

Something flashed out of the corner of my eye.

Lachlan. He cut through the water toward me, then grabbed the snake around the middle and yanked. The beast uncoiled as he dragged it off.

My mind buzzed, but one thought remained clear.

Get the sword.

I was almost out of breath, but this might be my only chance. Who knew how many snakes were in this lake, protecting the sacrifices?

I kicked toward the sword and grabbed the hilt, then shot to the surface. I broke through with a huge gasp, sucking in as much air as I could. The aching in my lungs subsided, and I stuck my head underwater, searching for Lachlan.

I spotted him about twenty yards away, snakeless and swimming for the surface.

Thank fates.

I surfaced, then kicked for the shore, cutting through the water toward the stone disc. By the time I reached it, my muscles were trembling from fading adrenaline. I crawled up onto the grass and flopped down.

Lachlan joined me.

"I thought St. Patrick drove the snakes from Ireland," Lachlan said.

"He did. But the Celts lived all over. I think this part of Otherworld represents somewhere else." The trembling in my limbs finally stopped. "What happened to the snake?"

"He disappeared as soon as you got the sword to the surface."

"Magic, then."

"Aye. They want to make this a challenge, it seems."

"We should work in pairs, then."

"Agreed."

I climbed to my feet and stumbled toward the stone disk, then set the blade into the proper indentation.

It fit perfectly, and a little jolt of magic shot up my arm as I set it down. I returned to Lachlan, who was standing in the shallows and staring out at the lake. I made a point not to look at his butt, though I really wanted to.

As I stopped beside him, he pointed toward a gleam of silver in the middle of the lake. "I think that's the shield."

"It's big enough."

"Aye. You go for it, I'll watch for snakes."

"Sounds like a plan." I waded into the water, glad to have Lachlan on my side.

Together, we swam out toward the gleaming shield. When it was right below us, I dived, cutting through the water quickly. Lachlan stayed at my side, his long arms making him look like a freaking Olympian.

The shield itself was decorated with swirls and red enamel. I reached for it. As soon as my fingertips made contact, a snake darted from behind a rock.

Lachlan was fast, grabbing the snake while I swam toward the surface. I broke through and sucked in a deep breath, then looked down and spotted Lachlan right as the snake disappeared.

Heck yeah.

He shot toward the surface. I started kicking for shore, dragging the heavy shield along. A few moments later, he joined me, reaching for my heavy cargo.

"I can handle it." Water nearly got in my mouth. Okay, maybe it was pretty heavy.

"Together."

I grinned, then let him grab one side of the shield. Together, we swam it to shore, then put it in the proper indention.

Finding the figurine took a bit longer, but it was the dagger that really gave us trouble. I grabbed a few off the bottom, but none of them seemed quite right. Worse, the snake never showed up, so they definitely weren't the correct daggers.

It took over an hour to pick up every one, and we devised a system that worked along a grid made from landmarks around the pond. Funny-shaped rocks and that kind of thing.

By the time I tested the last rock and it failed, frustration beat inside my chest. I shot toward the surface and sucked in a deep breath. Lachlan's head popped up near mine.

"It's not here," he said.

"Which sucks." I cut back toward shore, my mind racing. Had our target stolen it? And if so, was the path forever cut off to us?

Panting, I climbed onto shore and sat, staring at the lake. So many people had made sacrifices here over the years, and the one item that we still needed was gone.

Lachlan joined me, stretching out on the grass and staring at the sky. "What if it was never there to begin with?"

"The dagger?"

"Aye."

"Ah. So you think that *we* have to make a sacrifice."

"Seems likely."

I nodded. "I think you're onto something."

I scrambled up and shook myself off, trying to get as much of the water as possible off of me. Quickly, I pulled my clothes back on, then went to the stone disk. If Lachlan was right and this worked, I wanted to be dressed for whatever was coming next.

He followed, pulling on his clothes, and stopped at my side.

I stared down at the indention of the dagger. Suddenly, it looked familiar. It resembled one of my favorites, a gift from my sisters. I called on the dagger from the ether, then held it up for Lachlan to see.

"It's probably not always a dagger, but for me, it is."

"Aye, that'll be it."

I placed the dagger in the indentation. Magic fizzed up my arm, and I stood.

In front of me, the air shimmered.

I grinned. "It's working."

A delicate bridge formed over the lake. It looked like it was made of glass. Could we possibly walk on it?

The air on the other side of the lake cleared, revealing an enormous oak tree. It soared toward the sky, at least three hundred feet tall. The branches spread out so far that the thing was at least as wide as it was high.

"That has to be it," I said.

"The sacred grove? But there's only one tree."

"Maybe it's almost it." I stepped off the stone disk, leaving my dagger behind. Sadness tugged at me. I hated leaving it there, but that was the point of sacrifice, wasn't it? "Whatever the case, it's definitely the right direction."

I turned to look at the horses. They were way too big to make it over the skinny bridge.

"Bye, guys!" I waved at them.

They looked up and neighed, then turned and trotted off.

Lachlan followed, and we hurried across the bridge.

When I stepped onto the other side of the lake, magic enveloped me. It was comforting and warm, all the while making me slightly nervous. The feeling itched along my skin.

I looked at Lachlan, but before I could ask, he nodded. "Aye, I feel that."

"Strong, right?"

"Aye. This place is special."

I stepped toward the large tree, letting the magic wash over me. As I neared it, I spotted other trees. They seemed to come out of the mist. It felt like I was entering a land of dreams—hazy and vague.

"Keep going," the woods whispered.

I squinted at a tree trunk. Was that a face?

A figure drifted out from the trunk. She looked a bit like a ghost but tinged vaguely green and with rough, bark-like skin. A tree spirit.

"Keep going," she whispered. "You are not there yet. The way is long and dangerous."

I moved slowly through the woods, threading between the large trees as I followed the pull of my druid sense. Lachlan stuck by my side, but I barely noticed him. Every bit of my attention was glued to the forest around me.

At one point, the Cats of Catastrophe joined us, prowling along at my side.

The smell of fresh water filled the air, followed by the sound of a rushing river. I spotted it a moment later and hurried up to it.

A small boat sat against the shore, clearly waiting for me. It was tiny—big enough only for one. I turned to Lachlan and pressed a kiss to his mouth, then walked to the boat and stepped on. This was a journey that only I could make. I turned back to Lachlan.

Worry etched into his face. "Be careful."

I nodded. "I'll see you soon."

The boat pushed off from the shore, driven by magic. There were no oars or sail, just the pull of power.

Muffin meowed, *Hey! Hang on!*

"You can't—"

He sprinted away from the shore, then leapt onto the tiny boat. It rocked precariously. Princess Snowflake III and Bojangles followed, leaping off the shore to get onto the boat. Snowflake barely made it, her front paw grabbing onto the stern while her butt went in the water. She hissed and dragged herself on board.

Bojangles missed the boat entirely, but I was pretty sure that was on purpose. He swam alongside, his little head just above water and his goofy grin wide.

"Thanks, guys." I smiled, then gave Lachlan one last look.

I turned to look back at Lachlan. Behind him, a strange creature crept from the forest. It looked like a giant centipede, ten feet long at least. A shudder ran over me and I pointed. "Behind you!"

But he was looking at the river, a frown on his face. A splash sounded.

I turned to look.

Another centipede had slithered out from behind some bushes and into the river. It swam after me, its shiny eyes riveted to the boat.

Muffin meowed. *It wants to stop you.*

A third centipede emerged from the forest.

"Keep going!" Lachlan shouted to me. "I've got this."

"Alone?"

He just laughed confidently, then shifted into his lion form. His paws thundered on the ground as he raced toward the river and took a flying leap toward the centipede. The massive splash rocked my boat, and soon, he was wrestling with the beast, water flying all around.

Frustration seethed in my chest. Worry, too.

Muffin meowed. *You can't help him. This is his task. You must complete yours.*

I gritted my teeth as my boat drifted down the river, away from Lachlan. I watched him kill the centipede, his claws flying, then swim for shore. There were two more to deal with.

Something flashed in the forest. A third centipede.

One was already to the water. Lachlan went for him, lunging and driving him to the ground. He battled him in the shallows, water splashing.

Muffin meowed. *He's got this. You focus on what's ahead of you.*

Wherever I was going, it had to be me, alone. And Lachlan had my back.

7

As the boat slowly drifted away from the grove, the river entered a wide, flat field full of golden wheat.

Muffin meowed. *I've always hated boats.*

"Thanks for coming. You didn't have to."

We're a team. Of course I had to.

I reached down and scratched his head.

The boat continued to drift, floating past the fields that radiated a calm energy. It made my heart slow and my mind relax.

Shadows began to fill the air, floating alongside the boat. I blinked, squinting at them. My sisters? And my mother. Uncle Joe, from back in Death Valley. Anyone I'd ever loved followed along.

After a while, it seemed that we drifted through scenes of my past. Happy days with my mother. The horror of losing her to the bastards who'd hunted us. Lean days with my sisters, on the run. Finally making our way in Death Valley. Our first trip in the buggy, where we proved that we were as brave and strong as we'd always thought we were.

By the time we reached a split in the river, my mind was spinning from what I'd seen.

The boat stopped right before the river diverged into two. It hovered at the precipice of a decision.

My decision.

The left fork pulled toward answers. I could feel it as strongly as I could feel the wooden boat beneath my feet. If I went that way, it would be safe and comfortable and full of answers.

The other path…

The sound of a battle echoed from that one. Swords clanging, people screaming. No doubt, danger lay that way.

But also someone who needed me. I could *feel* it. Maybe it was my druid sense or just the nature of this place, but I knew that someone needed help. It'd be dangerous and take me off my path, but they *needed* me.

I looked down at Muffin.

He sighed, his little shoulders moving. *Really?*

"Yeah. I really think we need to go that way."

Of course you do.

I leaned right, directing the boat toward the battle. A prickling sensation skittered across my skin. Nerves. What would we face there?

The boat drifted down the right fork, headed toward the fight.

Muffin meowed. *Honestly, I think these are the trials that make you worthy of entering the sacred grove.*

"I have no idea what this is. Just that we need to go this way. Someone needs our help."

Fair enough.

I peered ahead, trying to spot what might wait for us. But all I could see was the river, winding ever onward. Anxiety pulsed in my chest, making my ribs feel too tight. The sound of the battle grew, but I could see nothing.

Finally, the boat beached itself on the side of the river, right below a hill. I scrambled out and raced up the hill, the cats at my side.

When I crested the top, I gasped.

Below, a battle raged. There were two factions. One was clearly made up of Celts. The other side was made up of Roman warriors, their armor gleaming in the sun.

Muffin meowed. *We're losing.*

We really were. There were two main sections to the battle. At the front, the Celts were trying to defend a village of round houses that sat behind them. The Romans pressed in, overwhelming them with greater numbers. It wouldn't be long before they overran the Celts and took over the village, killing or enslaving whoever was within.

There were Celtic reinforcements trying to reach their comrades, but they were blocked by a huge giant at a choke point between two rivers. The giant stood right in the middle, blocking the path to the battle. He swung a massive club, smashing anyone who tried to approach.

Without the reinforcements, the Celts would lose.

"We've got to stop that giant." I turned and raced back toward my boat.

Muffin meowed. *I like a challenge.*

I leapt onto the boat. There was no way I could beat my way through the army to reach the giant, so I had to attack from the side, using the river.

The cats followed me onto the boat, each making it on board easily this time, and the vessel pushed away from the shore. It continued downriver, and I willed it to go faster. We didn't have a lot of time.

The boat picked up speed as we moved, rushing through rapids that nearly threw me overboard. I crouched down and held on, the cats huddled around me. My own weird little army, but I wouldn't trade them for anyone.

My heart thundered as the sound of the battle increased. Shouts and moans, the clashing of blades. Soon, we were drifting by the horde of Celts who pushed toward the giant, trying to get past him at the choke point.

I drew a dagger from the ether and got ready to jump. The boat careened toward the choke point.

Muffin meowed. *Get ready!*

As if it followed my will, the boat veered left, toward land. Toward the giant, who stood on the little stretch of land between the two rivers, swinging his club toward the warriors who darted from the crowd. He took them out one by one, and the reinforcements didn't stand a chance.

The bow of the boat slammed into the dirt, and I jumped off, racing for the giant.

He turned to me, thirty feet tall and as wide as a semitruck. His ugly face looked like it'd been squished in by a brick. He roared and raised his club.

I am going to die.

The thought flashed in my mind, so bright and fierce that I knew it was true.

But the bodies of the fallen caught my eye. They'd raced forward, trying to dart past or take him out. All so they could get to the village and protect their friends.

I sucked in a deep breath and raced for the giant, the cats at my side. We had to take him out. There was no other option. If I could draw his attention for long enough, maybe they could sneak by.

The giant stepped toward me, his footsteps shaking the earth.

Muffin meowed. *We'll distract!*

The cats split up and raced ahead, circling the giant. He stopped and looked at them, confusion spreading across his face. I didn't blame him. It wasn't often you saw house cats who wore jewelry and were intent on killing you.

He swung his club for Bojangles, but the little cat was so fast that he leapt up onto the club itself, then lunged for the giant's head. He landed on the beast's nose, digging his claws in and holding on for dear life.

The giant howled and smacked at Bojangles, but he was too slow. The little orange cat scrambled onto the giant's head, digging in with his claws.

I took advantage of the distraction, trying to use my light magic to stop him. At first, I struggled. My tattoos made it hard, blocking my magic before it could leave me.

I have to save this village.

Finally, the light glowed from me, bright and fierce, but he was too big. Or too evil. Whatever it was, my magic wasn't working against him.

Crap.

I drew a dagger from the ether and hurled it at the giant's head. The steel plunged into his eye, and his roar shook my bones.

Yes!

Then he plucked the dagger out of his eye and turned to me, growling like a hellhound.

Oh, shit.

He didn't even look a little wounded.

Muffin and Princess Snowflake III went for his ankles, trying to distract him. I conjured another blade, this one longer, and darted left, trying to draw him toward my side of the river. If I could leave a gap between him and the other side, maybe some soldiers could sneak through.

The giant lumbered toward me, and fear chilled my skin. My weapons were too small.

I sucked in a deep breath and shoved the fear aside, then hurled my dagger.

He swatted it away.

Bojangles was attacking his head, but the cat was just too small to do any serious damage to a giant with skin as thick as an elephant's.

The giant swung his club for me, and I dived. Air whistled over my head as the club swung past, and I scrambled up.

The giant threw out his hand, shooting a blast of dark magic at me. It smelled of mildew and decay. I lunged left, barely avoiding it, and it plowed into the river behind me. In that one small area, the water grew deadly still, no longer flowing but not exactly ice, either.

What the hell was that magic?

I had no idea, and I didn't want to find out.

I needed something to take him down so I could get at his throat. Like a rope, or something.

A warrior in the crowd caught my eye. She stood at the perimeter of soldiers who watched us, her brow furrowed. At her waist, a whip was coiled.

I lurched toward her and reached out a hand, dodging a blow of the club before shouting, "Your whip! I need your whip!"

Her eyes flared wide, and she struggled to yank it off, then handed it over to me. I grabbed it and spun. The giant was lumbering toward me, club raised.

I sprinted around his left side, catching sight of Princess Snowflake III clinging to his leg, her claws dug deep into muscle. Bojangles was partway up his side, climbing toward the head. He'd probably fallen off, but he wouldn't give up.

"Bail out, guys!" I shouted.

The cats leapt off. Muffin sprinted toward me from the other side.

He meowed. *Give me an end!*

I tossed him the narrower end of the whip, and he gripped it in his teeth, then sprinted around the giant. The beast roared as he raised his club to smash my head in, not noticing the little cat that raced around his legs.

I held the whip handle in my left hand while I drew my dagger with my right, trying to keep his gaze on me. On the blade that I waved in the air like a moron. He didn't look too smart, and it seemed to work.

Panic thundered in my chest as I aimed and threw. The blade sank into his chest, but he hardly seemed to notice.

The giant raised a hand and threw another blast of dark magic at me. The scent of mildew and rot followed it through the air. I barely managed to dive left in time, and it plowed into the ground behind me.

Muffin had made a complete circle around the giant and was racing back toward me.

It was time.

I tugged the whip hard, yanking the giant's feet out from under him. He roared, crashing to the ground. A blast of his dark magic shot from his hand, but I didn't see where it landed.

I drew my sword from the ether and scrambled up on top of him, climbing over his belly like he was a small mountain. Before he could focus his eyes on me, I plunged my sword into his throat. Blood spurted. I yanked the blade to the right, determined to finish this.

The steel cut easily into his flesh. I yanked it around, doing as much damage as I could.

When a huge hand gripped me around the waist, shock dropped the world out from under me. Pain flared at my middle, greater than anything I'd ever experienced. The giant lifted me up and off him. Through bleary eyes, I could see that his own gaze was fading.

The arm holding me flopped to the ground, and I rolled out of his loose fist. Agony flooded me as I lay there, staring at the sky. I couldn't feel my limbs. And the battle had gone strangely silent.

Get up!

I tried to move my arms. My legs. But nothing worked. Finally, I managed to turn my head toward the giant, my head flopping onto the ground.

He lay still, staring at the sky through blind eyes.

I'd killed him.

Problem was, he might have killed me, too.

People surged around me, some racing for the battle on the other side of the path, others kneeling at my side and trying to help. The expressions on their faces said it all.

Something white caught my eye.

Princess.

She lay on her side, frozen and still. A woman was kneeling over her, a frown on her face.

No.

Princess must have been hit by the giant's dark magic. A blast of it had escaped him as he'd fallen.

Tears pricked my eyes. She couldn't be dead. Not one of my cats. She was frozen at the very least, some dark magic binding her limbs.

It took everything I had, but I managed the strength to move my arm toward her. I reached out my fingertips, calling upon the light inside me. It was partially a healing light, right?

I had to try.

I used what Lachlan had taught me—didn't even have to try, really. Of course I wanted to save Princess. The desire to heal her, to remove the dark curse, filled me. Sulis's light expanded in my chest, and gratitude for her help pounded in my heart. The light burst from my fingertips and shot toward Princess, making her glow golden and bright.

This was easier. Using it to heal rather than to maim. This felt natural.

Princess twitched.

Strength leached from my muscles.

All around, warriors ran. Those who surrounded me were growing quiet. Their lack of noise seemed to correspond with the fact that my vision was going dark.

I struggled to suck in a breath as I pushed my magic toward Princess. She moved her legs. Warmth filled me.

I gave her more magic, feeling the last of it slip through my fingers. As it did, she stood, hissing.

My vision went black.

I felt nothing.

In the distance, Muffin screeched.

8

Consciousness came slowly, though the world around me moved in a blur.

Warriors still streamed through the pass, and several people crouched around me, horror on their faces.

But it was the sight of Muffin's ugly mug hovering right over my own that really scared the crap out of me. He sat on my chest, staring down at me.

"What are you doing?" I croaked.

His green eyes widened. *Holy toadstools.*

"What?" I tried to shove him off me, but my hand went right through him.

What the hell?

I tried again, but my hand passed right through the cat. It was transparent. Like a ghost's.

Holy fates.

Had that giant killed me?

I sat up, feeling lighter than I ever had. As if gravity didn't bind me to the earth. But I wasn't floating like I would if I were in zero Gs.

So what the heck was going on?

The people around me didn't gasp or even acknowledge that I'd just risen from the dead. Their gaze stayed riveted to the ground. Where my real head probably was.

I'm not sure I'd look, if I were you. Muffin leapt to the side, and I had to assume he'd leapt off my body's chest, which was now slightly behind my head, since I was sitting up.

"As if I could resist." My stomach clenched as I turned, dreading what I would see.

I nearly hurled. Or I would have, if I weren't a ghost.

My body lay still and silent, my face unnaturally pale and my eyes wide open. A woman next to my head reached out and closed the eyes. I shuddered and turned.

"This isn't good," I said.

MTE. MTE.

"What does MTE mean?"

My thoughts exactly. Internet speak. Aren't you hip with the kids?

"No."

Well, I am.

Only then did I realize that Princess Snowflake III was staring at me with intense blue eyes. She head-butted my hip, which, for her, was a gesture of extreme affection. Bojangles was looking from my body to me, total confusion on his little face.

Slowly, I stood. It was weird to leave my body behind. Especially weird to be able to walk through people without anyone noticing.

Most of the warriors had rushed toward the battle and were now attacking the Romans, giving the original forces the backup they needed to save the town.

One of the warriors who'd sat around my body stood. "She was a hero."

"Just appeared out of the blue. Took out the giant no one else could."

Well, that was a high compliment. I looked at my body. Still dead though.

Muffin meowed. *We need to fix this.*

"I don't know how." But I still needed answers about what was happening with the three invaders. Just because I was dead didn't mean I could quit. Grief flashed through me briefly. If I couldn't fix this, I would lose my sisters.

I sucked in a deep breath.

Hell no.

I wasn't going to go down that path. It wouldn't help, and I had a job to do. Also, denial could work really well. "Well, I think we've finished here. Let's see if I can keep moving."

All right, Casper.

I scowled at Muffin, who grinned toothily at me. "You know, if I can't finish this job, you're going to have to."

Aye, aye, Captain.

The cats followed me to the boat. It was hard, but I managed to not look back at my body. It was too freaking weird. I didn't know what they'd do with me, and the idea kind of turned my stomach. Not that I thought they'd do anything bad. But even the idea of being buried....

Totally creepy.

The boat was waiting for us at the river, floating magically in place near the grass. I stepped on, and the cats followed me. Bojangles didn't even bother to jump onto the boat. He splashed right into the water and doggy-paddled—kitty-paddled?—alongside.

The boat took off, magic drawing it back down the river. It was surreal, really, knowing that I was on some kind of magical and divine journey as a ghost or spirit or whatever. I couldn't stop looking at my body, confirming that I was still dead.

Finally, I dragged my gaze away. The river wound through a field of golden wheat that blew gently in the air. To the left, a dark scar cut through the ground. It looked like the streak of evil that I'd been following, but worse. It plowed right through the earth, leaving a spray of dirt in its wake.

Muffin meowed. *That's bad news bears if I ever saw it. You're earning your way into the sacred grove. They're breaking in. Stealing.*

"Bastards."

Princess Snowflake III hissed. Bojangles paddled merrily along, having no idea that something was dreadfully wrong.

When my boat approached another grove of trees, excitement filled me. Normally, I'd hear the beat of my heart. Today, everything was silent. But this was it. I was close.

No question.

The boat pushed gently up to the shore, and I jumped off, followed by my sidekicks. Bojangles shook himself off, spraying me with water droplets that just flew through my ghostly form, then trotted ahead.

These trees were smaller than the other oaks, their bark silver and pale. They vibrated with magic, making me tingle with awareness.

When three figures stepped from the grove, shock raced through me.

The three shadows. They looked different than they had when they'd been fleeing from us in Italy after I'd torn their cloaks off, but their magic was the same. I'd never forget the stench or the prickle of unease.

On instinct, I darted behind a tree.

Princess Snowflake III hissed and Muffin meowed. *Someone got a makeover.*

He was right. They were still ephemeral, dark shadows that seemed to suck the light from the forest, but they were more solid now. I could make out features—they were definitely women, though their age was indecipherable. They wore clothes just like the attacking Roman soldiers I'd just seen on the battle-field. White cotton and golden armor.

That couldn't be a coincidence. I'd suspected before, but now I knew.

My enemy was Roman.

The Celts had fought the Romans for hundreds of years. I'd apparently been born to finish the job.

Or at the very least, keep it going.

"I've got to try," I whispered.

With what? You're a ghost. You going to scare them to death?

"If I can." I slipped out from behind the tree and followed them. I tried calling a dagger from the ether, but it didn't work. That spell had been attached to my body, not my soul.

They were walking away, their strides calm and sure. I called upon my magic, determined to blast them away with the golden light. I didn't know if it would work, but I had to try.

"Stop." The voice was quiet but resonated with power. A woman, I thought.

Shocked, my magic cut off abruptly. I turned. There was no one there.

"You can't kill them," the voice said. "Not in your state. Not with the magic you have now. But you *can* alert them to your presence. And that would be the end of you."

Frustration boiled within me. I turned to watch the retreating shadows. They were fifty yards away.

"Come. You must finish your journey and gain the magic that you came for. It is the only way you will succeed."

She—whoever she was—was right. I couldn't take them out with what I had currently.

I shoved aside the frustration and turned, walking deeper into the forest. My druid sense pulled me along, guiding me past trees and even a stone tomb decorated with skulls. Somehow I knew that they were the long decayed heads of ancient druids.

But that wasn't my destination.

Instead, I headed for an ancient-looking round house with a thatched roof. Smoke billowed from the middle of the roof, where I assumed a hole was cut to let it escape. The cats kept pace with me, padding silently along.

"Nervous?" I asked.

Muffin looked up at me, green eyes bright. *No. You?*

"Maybe a bit, yeah. What if they're like 'You? You're not who we expected.'"

Muffin meowed. *Don't forget that you earned your way here.*

Princess Snowflake III butted her head against my leg.

Bojangles burped.

I couldn't help the smile that tugged at my lips as I stepped through the door.

A woman waited within, standing behind the orange fire that burned in the middle of the empty house. She was clad in brown wool pants and a tunic. Leather armor lay against the wall, and her face was streaked with blood. Not her own, I thought, since I saw no wounds. She had a strong face and hard eyes that contrasted with the red hair that spilled down her back.

"Ana Blackwood," the woman said. "The Warrior Druid."

"Yes." After that, I drew a blank. Who was this woman?

"I am Boudica."

"Wow." She was the queen of the Iceni, a Celtic tribe of southern Britain, and the one who had nearly evicted the Romans from Britain. "I never thought I'd meet you."

"Likewise. But when you interceded on my behalf at the battle of Watling Village, it became obvious that I should be the one to meet you here."

"What do you mean?"

"Everyone must earn their way into the sacred grove." She scowled. "Well, almost everyone. But we will discuss that later.

When you were on the river, you had a choice of which direction to go. You could have come straight here, but you chose to go the long way, through the battle."

I nodded, not feeling the need to explain. She'd known why I'd done it. She'd sacrificed her life to lead a rebellion against injustice, after all.

"You put your life on the line," she said.

"And lost." I held up a transparent blue hand.

"You killed the giant. And saved your companion." She pointed to Princess Snowflake III, who was looking at her with a suspicious gleam in her eyes. "You could have saved yourself. Why didn't you?"

"Didn't occur to me."

"Not when your friend needed help. And you used up the last of your magic to save her. A rare choice." Her eyes shined with pride.

I felt vaguely awkward. I wasn't an idiot. I knew this was some version of a compliment. But I also wasn't good at taking those gracefully, so I kept my mouth shut. "Why were you fighting in your own afterlife? Was it a test for me?"

"Only in part. In many places, Otherworld is a mirror of the earthly realm, which means we fight battles occasionally. Even against the Romans, our greatest enemy. I continue to fight the battles that defined my life."

I wasn't sure if that was cool or sad.

"But this..." she continued. "This was different. The three who have invaded brought with them a dark energy that fueled their own kind."

"You mean it gave your Roman opponents more strength?"

"And viciousness. But we succeeded because of you and your sacrifice. It is what earned you your way here, and it is what will continue to earn you the magic that the gods will bestow upon you."

"What did the invaders find here? *Who* are they?"

"I don't know who they are, other than Roman. I call them The Three. It is a scared number, and I'm sure it is linked to their power."

"What did they get here? This place is for knowledge and power, correct?"

"They received both. Their bodies are stronger now. And they were looking for an army."

"For what?"

"I have no idea. But they found it. They will seek the Fomori. They are the most monstrous and evil beings in Celtic myth. Demons and dark gods. They can provide an army of immense power."

"Why would Romans want a Celtic army?" I asked.

"The Fomorian's would know that, not I."

If I made it out of here alive, that would be my next stop. "Can you tell me where to find them?"

"I imagine that your Undercover Protectorate would have some ideas. But you will need your magic first."

I looked down at my transparent body. "And a body."

She smiled. "That, we can accommodate. The Celtic soul is immortal. It is why you still walk despite the fact that your body has died."

"It has to help that I'm technically in the afterlife, right?"

"Indeed, it does. You will get your body back when you pass through the trials, which I have no doubt you will. Those same trials will also link your torc to your soul."

The necklace that Sulis had mentioned.

Boudica held out her hand, and a heavy golden necklace appeared. It was shaped like a C and very stiff, with an open space in the middle of one side. Ornate swirls twined around it.

"This is an ancient Celtic form of ceremonial jewelry that is normally worn by leaders."

My gaze travelled to the torc around her neck. It was heavy and strong, glowing golden in the light of the fire.

"The torc will allow you to understand and utilize the gifts that the gods bestow upon you. Once you wear it, they will begin to grant you their magic."

"I just have to pass through the trials."

"Precisely. Which I have no doubt you will do." She held out the torc, shaking it slightly to make her intentions clear.

I stepped forward quickly and grabbed the torc, my ghostly hand not stopping me from holding it. Power zinged up my arm as my fingertips closed around the gold. I inspected it. The swirls of metal were actually part of a dragon. It twined around the necklace, looking fierce.

"This is amazing."

"Put it on."

I slipped the torc around my neck. Magic zipped through me as it settled heavily against me. Though I was in my ghost form and couldn't touch anything else, *this* didn't care about such silly rules. It felt like it would stick with me no matter what. I reached up to touch it. The torc was smooth and cool beneath my fingertips.

Then it began to heat.

My eyes flashed to Boudica. "What's—"

Pain flared, bright and brief. It was gone a second later. So was the torc. The golden necklace no longer rested heavily around my neck. But the skin around my neck felt different. Almost like it vibrated with magic.

"It's become part of you," Boudica said. "That way, you'll never lose your gifts. Or your ability to use them."

That sounded pretty good, actually. And I definitely felt different. Like something inside of me had calmed down. Before this, my magic had been a crazy carnival and most of the carnies had been asleep on the job. Now, it was orderly and precise. I bet if I tried, I could use any of my magic now without issue.

Boudica held out her hand again, and a tiny torc rested there. "Your familiar has earned one as well."

Muffin meowed and sauntered forward. He sat regally on his butt—don't ask how it was possible, but he managed it—and stared up at her with his wrinkled face. She placed the torc around his neck, and he purred.

Briefly, it glowed bright, then it disappeared into him as well. A golden tattoo traced over his shoulders, looking like the twisted torc.

"Cool," I said. "What does—"

Wings sprouted off Muffin's back, little silver things that sparkled in the firelight. He jumped, surprised, and looked back.

I'd once imagined him with wings, and here he was. My winged, hairless, magical Cat Sìth. What a weird life I led.

Princess Snowflake III sniffed him suspiciously, while Bojangles licked his butt in the corner, oblivious to all that was going on around him.

Muffin took a running start, sprinting across the small roundhouse. He crouched low on his powerful hind legs and took off, little wings carrying him into the air.

They didn't take him far—only a few feet—but when he landed, he looked very pleased with himself.

"Well done," I said. "And you'll probably get even better."

Boudica shot me a look that suggested this was as good as it was going to get, but Muffin looked so pleased with himself and his little wings that it didn't matter.

Boudica looked at Princess Snowflake III. "And you as well."

Princess strolled forward and sat, preening as Boudica put the torc around her neck. As soon as it disappeared, Princess shot a blast of fire from her mouth. She looked pleased with herself after that.

Boudica gestured to Bojangles, who looked around like *who, me?*

"Yes, you small strange cat."

Bojangles gamboled forward, then rolled over onto his back right in front of her.

"I'm not sure that's how it's supposed to be done, Bojangles," I said.

"It's fine." Boudica slipped a tiny torc around his neck. A moment later, he disappeared.

"Oh, that's gonna be dangerous," I muttered.

A moment later, Bojangles appeared on the other side of the room.

Muffin purred with delight. *We'll be able to steal* everything.

I sighed but didn't correct him. Not like I could control him anyway. I looked at Boudica. "The gods really trust me with their magic?"

She nodded. "They do. You were born worthy, Ana. Your soul was a beacon for the gods, making it clear that you would do the right thing with your powers. They cannot walk the earth anymore, helping those in need. But *you* can. And you've proven yourself willing throughout your life. Brave and selfless, kind and generous. It is you who are worthy of their magic. Now that you have the torc, you'll be able to use what they give you." Her face turned grim. "And I think you may need it. I couldn't stop The Three who came here earlier, but someone must. Their magic is dark, and their intentions darker. I think they are tied to you somehow. Your fate meshed with theirs."

"This was meant to be," I said. "The Celts fought the Romans in ancient times, and I'm meant to do it again."

"Aye, I think that's right." Intensity gleamed in her eyes, almost vicious. "You *must* win. *Beat* them, Ana. For all of us."

Flashes of history passed through my mind, memories of reading about Boudica. Her daughters had been killed in a

Roman attack, and she'd picked up the sword to rouse the Celts in a revolt against the invaders from the south. She'd nearly won, too.

But she hadn't. She'd died a tragic death instead.

Of course she wanted vengeance on the Romans.

"I'll stop them," I said. "Whatever they want, they won't get it."

She nodded, satisfied. "Good. Now there's one more thing. You will leave here and pass through the trials to get your body back. I don't know what they will be, but they'll be linked to you somehow. And not easy."

"I can do it."

She grinned. "I like confidence in a person."

I saluted. "I got it in spades."

I might not have always been confident in my magic—having defensive magic in an offensive world had sucked—but I was confident in my ability to suck it up and do what was necessary. To keep pushing and trying until the job was done. Plans A, B, and C would get me there eventually.

"Best of luck to you, Ana," Boudica said. "I think you're going to need it."

9

B oudica disappeared, and I turned, ready to face whatever the trials were.

When the flame burst to life around me, I stumbled back, shocked. But the flames rolled toward me, fiercely hot.

Frantic, I looked around for the cats. "Run!"

They arched their backs and hissed at the flame. I turned back to it. The flickering orange tongues of heat had crept closer. The burning was so intense that it made my eyes water. I stepped back, away from it.

Muffin meowed. *I wouldn't do that if I were you.*

Fear flowed through me as I turned.

More flame.

So much flame.

So much heat.

My skin began to burn, so hot that it would have melted if I'd been more than a ghost. I might not have had a real body, but apparently my nerve endings still worked just fine.

The flame was nearly to me now, only a few feet away on all sides. The burning increased, so powerful I could have fallen over.

What am I supposed to do?!

There was no way out. Just a world of fiery death.

I sucked in a deep breath and stiffened my spine. My knees were about to go out from under me, so it was no easy task, but I managed. The air in my lungs was so hot, I almost couldn't bear it.

We had to get out of here. I had to get my cats out of here. They were hissing, and pissed as hell. Even Bojangles was paying attention to his surroundings.

The heat was so bad that it felt like it reached inside me, burning muscle and bone. It was one with me, so ferocious that it filled me up, making me feel like the fire itself.

My collarbones burned, my shoulders lighting up with pain. The area around my lower neck hurt the worst by far. Then it didn't.

The torc?

Use it, a voice whispered. *The flame is yours.*

I jerked. Whoa.

Was this magic mine?

Could it be?

Through the horrible pain, I tried to focus on the fire. Tried to feel for a core of magic that I could manipulate and use. If I wanted to get out of this, I would have to bend this flame to my will.

The fire danced around me at first, alighting on me only to cause pain. I sucked in a deep breath and focused. It wasn't hard to imagine why I wanted to use this magic. I really didn't want to burn to death.

Finally, I caught the tail end of it. The fire that had begun to flicker within my belly was *mine.* I commanded it, driving it away. Visions of the flame sweeping away from me flashed in my mind, and the fire obeyed. It rushed backward, leaving me and the cats standing and panting. The pain faded.

Took you long enough.

I looked at Muffin.

His annoyed green eyes met mine. *Almost singed my new wings.* He fluttered the little things.

Princess Snowflake III just hissed at me, clearly having forgotten that I'd just saved her life. Ah, well, I was more comfortable with her ire anyway.

Bojangles had somehow managed to capture a little ball of flame and was now playing with it. The glow of fire lit up his eyes as he tossed it back and forth between his paws.

I left him to it and stepped forward, determined to get these trials over with. I was still a ghost, so there was clearly more to go through.

The round house had burned down, revealing the silver trees that filled the sacred grove. It was so calm and pretty that when a massive wind rushed through and picked me up, it took half a second to process what was happening.

By then, the wind had swept me up above the trees. Far below, the cats stared up at me, shock on their little faces.

Hang on! I'm coming! Muffin leapt off the ground, his little wings carrying him slowly up toward me. He huffed and puffed to get higher, and in the meantime, the wind tossed me around like a rag doll, dropping me and picking me back up again. My heart leapt into my throat and my extremities went numb. I nearly slammed into the trees twice, and I knew without a doubt that if I did, I'd be dead.

Trial failed, body gone.

Forever.

Muffin huffed his way to me, flying slightly above me and grabbing the back of my jacket with his claws. I could almost hear his little wings fluttering frantically.

Got you!

I dipped again on a current, not quite as quickly as before.

Muffin was buying me some time and a bit of stability, but the little cat couldn't carry someone as big as me.

The wind tossed us around as Muffin tried to keep me aloft.

You better think of something quick! You weigh as much as a prize tuna!

"Always with the tuna."

Always.

I sucked in a deep breath and focused on the wind that tossed me around. If this was anything like the fire, it could be part of me. I could control it.

The wind itself was cold and sharp, a contrast to the flame that would have melted me like an old tire if I'd had a body. It flowed around me, even through me, in my transparent form.

I grabbed onto it, feeling it like a physical thing in my hands. It was more than just particles of oxygen and nitrogen, it was *mine*.

Magic flowed through me, starting at my torc, and the wind began to obey my commands. It stopped tossing me around, and instead, it allowed me to slowly lower myself to the ground.

I was nearly there when the wind disappeared entirely, and I splashed into water. The liquid closed around me, cold and wet. Shock lanced me as I kicked for the surface. I broke through, struggling and spitting.

Desperate, I sucked in a lungful of air and kicked, trying to keep my head above water. The cats were nowhere to be seen, and I prayed they weren't part of this trial.

A huge wave crashed down over me, pushing me deeper into this new sea. The water thrashed around me, pushing me deeper and deeper.

It was cold and dark all around, threatening to crush me in the darkness. My lungs burned and my mind screamed.

Trapped.

I struggled for the surface but made no progress. Panic

threatened to overwhelm me, dragging me down into a pit of despair.

I fought it with everything I had.

And then I didn't.

Maybe I shouldn't fight it. It wasn't doing me any good or getting me anywhere. Maybe the water was part of me.

On instinct, I opened my mouth and sucked in. Water flowed into my mouth, my lungs. But it didn't hurt.

Far from it.

Strength and energy filled me. The water around me became a friend. Or at least something that wasn't out to hurt me.

I kicked upward, easily finding my way to the surface. My head broke through, and I sucked in air, then commanded the water to disappear.

It did, dropping me into the dirt.

The cats appeared around me.

Muffin gave me an unimpressed look. *You look rough. You see any tuna?*

"No tuna. And I feel rough. But apparently I'm a mermaid." Or the closest thing to it.

I'll believe it when I see it.

Something soft hit me on the head. I looked up. A dark splotch in the air was headed right for me. A millisecond later, a clod of dirt hit me in the face.

Sputtering, I backed up, shaking the dirt away. More began to fall, hitting the top of my head and piling around me. Bojangles chased it, but the other cats hissed, trying to avoid the dirt.

You better do something about this!

It was already up around my waist. Shit.

More fell, faster and faster. It would bury me alive, and somehow I knew that there was no way I'd be able to breathe in dirt.

Forever.

No thanks.

I sucked in a deep breath and called upon my magic. My neck burned, right where the torc had absorbed into me. A moment later, I swore I could feel the dirt around me. Like it was an extension of me.

I commanded it to stop, visualizing the sky becoming clear again. Magic flowed through me, out into the world, wrapping around the dirt and commanding it to halt.

A moment later, the sky cleared. No more dirt.

Next to me, Muffin was buried up to his neck. So were Princess Snowflake III and Bojangles. They must have had to scramble to stay above the dirt as it fell.

They looked at me, clearly annoyed.

About time.

I scrambled out of the dirt pile that had formed around me, reaching down and pulling out the cats one by one. Snowflake was the biggest mess, her white fur a total disaster. She hissed at me.

"Sorry, sorry."

I turned to figure out what the hell would come next, and I spotted Lachlan. The dirt had disappeared, and so had the sacred grove. I stood at the edge of the river where I'd left him. The land around him was torn up, as if he'd been battling centipedes for hours, their thrashing limbs tearing up the grass and dirt.

But there were no more monsters, and he looked fine.

Shock and relief flashed across his face. I felt the same, deep in my bones.

"Thank fates," he said.

My boat pressed up against the shore, and he tugged me into his arms, hugging me tight.

I startled.

Hugging *me.*

I had a body again.

I whooped and hugged him back, gratitude flowing through me.

Lachlan pulled back and looked at me, his dark eyes concerned. "Are you all right?"

"Definitely. It was a bit touch-and-go for a moment there, but I'm doing good now. I got my powers. Or at least, some of them."

He grinned, and kissed me hard and fast. "Well done."

"But how are you? How many centipede monsters were there?"

"Couple dozen. They were meant to stop you."

"But you stopped them. Thank you."

"Any time." He pressed another kiss, this one to to my forehead.

"We need to get back to the Protectorate. I've got info we need to hunt down. I know where we need to go next."

He kissed me on the forehead. "I can only imagine that it will be dangerous."

"Oh, you're imagining right."

It wasn't hard to get back to the Protectorate. As if Otherworld had realized that I'd accomplished my goal already, it had spit us out pretty much immediately, and we found ourselves standing on the lawn in front of the castle. One second we were in Otherworld, the next, we were in Scotland.

The sun was dipping behind the horizon and the night air growing chilly. I'd lost all track of time in Otherworld, but it was evening here.

Immediately, I pressed my fingertips to my comms charm. "Bree? Rowan? Where are you?"

Bree's voice filtered through. "We're at the Whisky and

Warlock. Jude's here too. Most people, really."

"We'll be right there." My stomach rumbled as loud as a truck, no doubt at the thought of the meat pie that the pub served. I was famished.

"Dinner time?" Lachlan asked.

"Is it ever. Let's go eat and talk."

We made our way quickly through the enchanted forest, passing by the gnarled old trees and the fairy lights to find the portal that would take us to Edinburgh. I let the portal suck me through the ether and spit me out in the alley in the Grassmarket. The sound of revelry echoed from the main street.

Lachlan and I pushed through the crowd, which seemed to be celebrating some kind of sports victory, if the matching outfits were any indication, and made our way into the Whisky and Warlock.

I turned left, entering the room that was usually full of Protectorate members. The fire burned merrily in the hearth, and Sophie wiped down the bar, a big grin on her face. The smell of food and beer made my stomach grumble, while the scent of woodsmoke made me want to sink down in a chair in front of the fire and never get up. Apparently, my trials in the Otherworld had given me a powerful need for a nap.

"Ana!" Rowan's voice cut through the crowd.

I turned, catching sight of her by the bar with Bree. I hurried toward them. They threw their arms around me in a big hug. Before I'd even pulled away, I blurted, "I found our mother."

Rowan pulled back and gasped. "What?"

Shock flashed on Bree's face. "Where? Otherworld?"

"Yep. She lives there now. It's her afterworld."

"Oh my gosh." Tears sprang to Bree's eyes.

"You can take us to see her?" Rowan asked.

I grinned, happier than I'd ever been in all my life. "Yep."

"Wow. I just..." Bree shook her head. "I can't believe it."

"This is amazing." Happiness glowed from Rowan.

"Ana!" Jude's voice echoed across the bar.

I turned, catching sight of her at a table by the mullioned windows. She sat with Caro, Ali, and Haris. Hedy sat at the end, along with Jessie Ammons, head of the Demon Trackers Unit.

"Let's go," I said. "We'll catch up more about mom later."

"Definitely," Bree said.

We headed toward them and gratefully took the seat that offered. Lachlan sat next to me, and my sisters squeezed in at the end.

"You look like you could use some chow," Ali said.

"Definitely."

He stood. "You hang out. I'll get you something. Meat pie or fish and chips?"

"Pie."

Lachlan nodded his agreement.

"And water," I added. "No time to celebrate yet. I'll save the champagne for when we finish this."

Jude's eyes searched mine. "So you've found something? What's going on in Otherworld?"

"It's more than we realized," I said. As quickly as I could, I explained the issue with The Three invading Otherworld in search of an army.

"So they're the *same* people you fought last week and that Lachlan has been hunting?" Jude sat back and rubbed a weary hand over her face. "I don't like the coincidence."

"Dangerous," Jessie rumbled.

I rarely heard the big blond man speak, and it sounded like he could eat glass.

"I don't think it's a coincidence," Hedy said. "We definitely shouldn't assume that it is."

Ali delivered our food and water at that moment, apparently having sweet-talked Sophie into getting it quickly. I chowed down, trying not to eat like a ravenous bear. But it was so danged good. I was also starving, so that probably had something to do with it.

"So you need to go to the land of the Fomori?" Caro looked at me with wide eyes and whistled. "Dangerous."

I swallowed the last bite of pie. "Jealous?"

"A bit." She grinned. "I'd love to see it."

"Unfortunately, you won't," Jude said. "It's nearly impossible to get there, and we can only send two at most."

"Lachlan and I will do it." I didn't know if Jude had already been considering that, but I wanted in on this mission no matter what. "I gained the rest of my powers in Otherworld, so I'm qualified. And I want to see this through. This is all linked to me somehow. I know it."

Jude nodded. "I agree. It's no coincidence. And this isn't finished yet. The druids said they needed the two of you." She pointed between Lachlan and me. "The Fomori are Celtic demons. It's all linked, and you're part of it."

"How do we get there?" I asked. "Boudica mentioned that the Protectorate would know."

"We do, and it was difficult to get the info. But we have a contact who can get you in, though it won't be easy. The realm of the Fomori is in the Atlantic Ocean."

"In? Like, *under*?" I asked.

"The closest thing to Atlantis," Lachlan said. "But full of demons. There's a bubble around it, so you won't need gills."

"So we'd be trapped underwater with a bunch of demons, unable to escape if we got separated from our ride," I said.

"Pretty much." Jude nodded. "It's not for the faint of heart."

"Not a problem." I sipped my water. "How do we get in?"

"There are two entrances that we know of. One in Dublin, through the river Liffey, and another through New York."

"New York?" Lachlan asked. "That's far from Celtic turf."

"Lots of Irish moved to New York. And Celtic culture has never been about place," Jude said.

"Fair point." Lachlan nodded.

"We're going to have to get in touch with our contact," Jude said. "It's not always easy to find him. Once we do, you'll go and meet him. He'll get you in, but he won't go past the gate. When you're in the realm of the Fomori, you'll seek out our undercover man."

"Jonnie." Ali grinned. "I wonder how the bastard is doing?"

"Probably smells like fish by now," Haris said.

"Who is Jonnie?" I asked.

"He works with my unit," Jessie said. "A demon tracker. He's been undercover in the realm of the Fomori for six months now."

"So, before we showed up here," Bree said.

"Exactly. The Fomori shouldn't be leaving their realm and coming to earth. But they are, in too many numbers. Jonnie is there trying to figure out why and how."

"And he'll help us find out who The Three are looking for?" Lachlan asked.

"He'll try," Jude said. "In the meantime, get a bit of rest. We'll find out where Shen is—that's our contact in New York—then you'll head there immediately."

"I'll go to help," Bree said.

"Me too," Rowan added.

"Sorry." Jude shook her head. "Like I said, Shen can only take two at a time. It's not an easy journey."

Bree and Rowan scowled but nodded.

I smiled my thanks at them, wishing they could come. I'd been spending more time away from them lately, and our favorite thing to do together was kick ass and take names. But given the threat that The Three posed, we'd probably have a chance to do that sooner rather than later.

Because Jude needed some time to locate Shen, we had a few hours to sleep. My feet dragged up the stairs toward my tower apartment, but my skin prickled with awareness. Lachlan walked behind me. There wasn't enough time for him to go back to his place and get rest, so it'd been the most obvious thing to invite him back to my place.

As soon as I walked in, I went to the bathroom to check out my new tattoo in the mirror. I tugged aside my shirt collar and peered at it. The markings were much fainter than the ones around my arms, a pale gold that shimmered in the light.

Swirls of gold danced over my collarbones, and if I squinted, it looked like a dragon.

"Cool." I spared one look for my face and winced.

Yeah, I needed a nap. I looked as ragged as a superstore employee after Black Friday. I'd never personally attended a Black Friday sale, what with living in the desert and being broke, but I'd heard stories. It sounded more exhausting than driving across Death Valley.

"Help yourself to anything!" I shouted out to Lachlan, belatedly realizing that I'd just ditched him. "I'm going catch a shower."

"Aye." His voice filtered through the door.

Quickly, I scrubbed up, then changed into PJs and went down the stairs toward the kitchen. Lachlan handed me a warm mug.

I smiled. "What is this?"

"Hot chocolate. Found it in the back of your cupboard."

"The only thing the cats haven't eaten."

"Though they might have tried?"

"Bojangles, definitely. That cat's got a sweet tooth like you wouldn't believe." I sipped and sighed gratefully. "You know the way to a girl's heart."

"I wouldn't mind finding my way to *your* heart, specifically."

I smiled at him, my heart thundering. But I had no idea what to say, so I went with silence.

He squeezed my arm and set his mug on the counter. "I'm going to take a shower."

"You do that. I'm hitting the hay. You can, um, join me when you're done." I held up a hand. "Sleeping only, though. We've only got a few hours at most, and we need it."

The corner of his mouth kicked up in a devastatingly sexy smile, and he nodded.

I listened to him go up the stairs and waited for the water to start. Once I'd finished my hot chocolate, I climbed into bed. Softness enveloped me. Felt like sinking into a cloud.

I drifted into sleep almost immediately. Vaguely, I felt Lachlan climb into bed next to me, and I rolled toward him, snuggling into his arms.

I could get used to this.

～

Jude found Shen by three a.m. We woke when she called, then dressed and stumbled down the stairs toward the main entry hall. Muffin led the procession, flying along and bumping into things.

When we arrived, Jude eyed us skeptically. "You look tired."

"I feel okay." I scrubbed a hand across my eyes. I really did feel a lot better after the five hours of sleep. Despite the godawful time, Jude looked pressed and perfect, as always, and ready to kick ass.

"You ready?" she asked.

"As I'll ever be," I said. "Where'd you find the guy?"

"A place called the Jade Tiger in New York City's China Town. You'll find it down Supe Alley, where most of the supernaturals congregate."

"China Town?"

"He's a Chinese dragon shifter."

"Whoa. And he's supposed to get us to a land from Celtic myth?"

She shrugged. "New York is a melting pot. If you went through Dublin, you'd probably ride a Kelpie to get there."

I nodded. "All right, then. We're off to China Town."

"Be careful," Jude said. "And do whatever Shen tells you. The realm of the Fomori is one of the most dangerous places there is. Missteps are not forgiven there."

"We'll be careful." I tried to smile reassuringly.

"Good. I don't want to lose you." She gave us a nod, then walked off. No doubt to go to bed. Or to kick some demon ass, knowing Jude. Who knew what she got up to at this hour?

Lachlan and I swung by the kitchen to grab a to-go breakfast before heading out. Boris, the little rat, was curled up on a pillow in front of the fire. He loved food so much that he pretty much never left the kitchen, but he had excellent manners and only ate off of tiny plates designated specifically for him. I wanted to pet his head as I passed his sleeping spot but resisted for fear of waking him up. He was so cute that I couldn't bear it.

Hans had left wrapped-up sandwiches in the fridge, along with an army of juice boxes. I grabbed one of each and followed Lachlan back up the stairs, eating as I walked.

When we reached the courtyard outside, the night was frigid. A slender moon glowed faintly in the sky above, and we polished off our sandwiches.

"Ready?" Lachlan asked.

"Ready."

He held out his hand, and his magic surged on the air. The portal appeared, and I stepped in, letting the ether suck me through space and spit me out on the other side of the world. I appeared in a darkened alley, thankfully. It'd be no good to pop out of thin air in front of a non-magical person.

While I waited for Lachlan, I headed toward the alley exit, peering out onto the street.

It was busier here since it was only about ten p.m. Cars zipped down the street, and revelers stumbled from bar to bar, while restaurants served a few last stragglers a late meal. I didn't see anyone that I would pinpoint as a supernatural, though I caught a whiff of some magical signatures that definitely weren't normal New York City smells. The scent of fresh honeysuckle, for one.

Lachlan appeared next to me a moment later.

"Where are we exactly?" I asked.

"Near China Town and Supe Alley. This is my normal entry point for New York, so I figured it was safest."

"Your favorite grungy alley?" I grinned.

"Gotta have one in every city." He took my hand and pulled me out onto the street.

But he didn't let go.

I smiled and squeezed tighter. Sure, we were on a job and

this was dangerous. But that was basically my whole life. So if I didn't steal a little romance when I had the chance, I'd never get it.

It was obvious when we made our way into China Town. Pretty paper lanterns decorated the street, and the scent of delicious food wafted on the air. Despite my sandwich, my stomach rumbled again. There was a mishmash of shops—some selling traditional goods like herbs and others that sold more touristy stuff.

Lachlan cut confidently through the crowd as if he knew right where we were headed.

"You've been here before?" I asked.

"Not to Jade Tiger but to Supe Alley, yes. Great place to buy potion ingredients that I can't grow."

I eyed a fascinating shop full of thousands of little glass bottles of herbs. "I can imagine."

A few minutes later, we turned onto Supe Alley. At first, I thought it was just a dead end crowded with old dumpsters. Definitely not an inviting place, but that was the point. Had to keep the humans out somehow.

Lachlan clutched my hand and dragged me straight through a dumpster. Magic prickled against my skin as I passed through, and the lovely scent of incense filled my nose. I grinned. Someone had apparently given the dumpster doorway a nice magical air freshener.

There was one last crackle of magic as we passed through the dumpster doorway, and we were in Supe Alley.

The change in the air was immediate and intense. Magical signatures abounded, everything from the pretty sound of bells to the stench of old socks.

Here, there were shifters with their tails out and fairies letting their wings flow in the breeze. Supernaturals who looked a little different tended to love places like this, where they could be themselves without worrying about catching the attention of humans.

"I don't think the shop is located at this end of the street," Lachlan said. "I've been here a few times and never seen it."

"Let's head farther down, then."

We made our way through the crowd, artfully dodging the people who filled the streets. The scent of food was just as strong back here, and even more delicious if possible. A group of women in beautiful silk dresses passed by us. The dresses looked like some kind of traditional garment, but for the life of me I wouldn't have been able to come up with a name.

I liked this place, though. So much of our lives had been spent hanging out in crappy little towns like Death Valley Junction or living in the wilds of Alaska with our mom. I hadn't had a chance to see much of the world, and this was pretty danged cool.

Yet another thing to thank the Protectorate for. With them, I got to see so much.

"I think we're getting close," Lachlan murmured. He pointed to a building up ahead. It was darker, with two guards out front, each wearing a fancy suit.

"How do you know?"

"That place looks like trouble, and that's how our luck tends to run."

I cracked a smile and wasn't surprised when I caught sight of the sign over the place. Jade Tiger.

"Bingo," I said.

We approached the door and the guards. I couldn't see a weapon on them, but in the supernatural world, that didn't mean anything.

"What do you want?" one of the guards grunted.

"We're here to see Shen," I said.

"Hmmmpf." Both guards scowled at us, then stepped aside and opened the two ornately carved doors.

Lachlan and I entered a room that was dimly lit and mysterious. No joke, if someone had looked up *mysterious* in the dictionary, this place would have had its picture right under the word.

The air smelled strongly of some type of herb, with the faint trace of antiseptic beneath. Smoke twisted through the air like a dragon, sinuous and smooth as it twined around the tables and chairs.

On one side of the room, people sat at the little tables, playing games. They chatted in low voices, the energy relaxed yet somehow still slightly tense. It was so weird that it made my skin itch.

On the other side of the room, the faint buzz of machinery was overlaid by a live band. Spotlights gleamed on people sitting in chairs. I squinted, trying to figure out what was happening over there.

"Wait, is this a tattoo parlor?" I asked. It was strange, given that the place had the feeling of a cool gambling den.

"I think so," Lachlan said.

"Can I help you?" An older woman approached, her hair streaked with gray. She wore a sleek black suit and had eyes that were sharp as glass. They landed on my collarbones. "That's quite the piece of artwork you have there."

I reached up to touch the tattoo that glowed faintly on my skin. It wasn't noticeable to most people, at least I didn't think it was, given how faint it had been in the mirror. But this lady had an eye for tattoos, I had to imagine.

"Yes. It's special to me." I left it at that, hoping she wouldn't pry. "Is Shen here? We're looking for him."

"Hmmm." She scowled at us. "My son keeps the worst company."

"Hey! I'm not that bad," I said.

"Maybe not you, but he is." She pointed to Lachlan. "And don't even get me started on your cat."

Her gaze dropped to something behind me, and I turned to see Muffin sitting there, shooting the woman a toothy grin.

"Don't smile at me," she said to him. "I know it was you who stole my jade necklace."

Muffin put on a fake innocent expression that was the worst I'd ever seen. I could just see him dragging the necklace out of her bedroom. I'd have to have a talk with him.

I looked her. "I'll make him return it. I promise."

She gave me a hard look, then nodded. "See that you do. Now, come this way."

We followed her to a door in the back. I shot Muffin a couple of disapproving glares. "You really need to return that."

He wouldn't look at me.

"*Muffin!*"

He glared at me. *Fine.*

"Good. I know I can't change you, but don't steal from people who help us."

She wasn't helping us then.

I rolled my eyes.

The woman pushed open the door, leading us into a room with slightly better light.

It was the most fabulous library I'd ever seen, second to the one at the Protectorate, of course. Though it wasn't huge, the shelves on the walls were packed full of books and scrolls. There had to be thousands of books in here, their spines illuminated by the golden light shining from the lamps. But it was the scrolls that caught my eye. They gleamed, pale white and cream, and I itched to open one up and see what was inside.

I had a feeling I'd never get the chance, though. Iron statues stood guard in the room, positioned in front of the shelves. They looked like the Terracotta warriors but made of metal. I'd bet big bucks that if I touched a single book without permission, they'd come alive and jump me.

A movement from the back of the room caught my eye, and I turned to look. A young man stood there, his form slim and his eyes dark. His hair was expertly cut in a sweep across his forehead, and he'd look like a young movie star if it weren't for the hardness on his face and the aura of danger that surrounded him.

"Yes?" His voice was cold.

"Shen, these people are here to see you," his mother said. "Be nice."

He gave her a look that was somehow loving and exasperated while still holding on to that cold edge. Then he turned to us and scowled. "What do you want?"

"We're here from the Undercover Protectorate. We were told you could help us get into the realm of the Fomori."

His face softened just slightly, and when he spoke, there was something heavier in his voice. Almost like longing, though I felt crazy for thinking it. "Jude sent you?"

"She did."

He nodded, most of the coldness fading from his face. He looked like a different person now. Still not someone I'd want to mess with, but he didn't look like he'd make a snack out of my heart anymore, at least.

I heard the door shut behind me and realized that his mother must have left. "What is this place?"

"Family business."

"Doing what?" As soon as the words were out of my mouth, I realized I shouldn't have asked them. "I mean, this is a great library."

"Knowledge is power."

That was true. And while I had no idea what these folks did, they clearly had a lot of power.

"How do we get to the realm of the Fomori?" Lachlan asked.

"First, you pay. And it won't be cheap."

"That's fine." Lachlan stepped forward and pulled out his wallet.

While he made the transaction, I inspected the shelves, my fingertips itching. It was so danged hard not to reach for one of the volumes, but I was used to not getting what I wanted. I squeezed my hand into a fist.

"Now that that is settled, we can get down to business," Shen said. "I can give you a ride to the main gate of Fomori. But once there, I won't enter. You're on your own. You'll need a disguise, though."

I shuddered at the memory of the nasty, dark-magic soaked cloaks we'd had to wear when looking for Grimaldi's. *Please not that.* "We don't have to pretend to be Fomorians, do we?"

"No. And you wouldn't pass even if you tried. Your best bet is pretending to be traders. Go in with something so valuable they won't turn you away."

"Any suggestions?" Lachlan asked.

"Energy stones. They're always looking for more power down there. It's not easy keeping an underwater world running. Electricity doesn't do so hot underwater. Same with the fumes from gas engines. And there's no sun. So they rely on energy stones, but they're in short supply."

"That sounds like a good plan. Where would we get some?" I asked.

He grinned, and it was vaguely shark-like. "I can help you there. They're expensive, though, and rare. I can only spare two, so you'll go in with some fake ones as well. If you get stopped by guards, show them the real ones and hope they don't check the rest."

"What happens if they do?"

"You don't want to know."

After getting us each kitted out with a leather bag full of stones and some hats that looked like Indiana Jones rip-offs, Shen led us out of Jade Tiger and onto the main street.

"I have a preferred entry point at the river," he said. "We'll go there, then get started."

"How are you taking us?" He hadn't mentioned before.

"I'm a dragon shifter." He gave me a look and raised his brows.

"A sea serpent?" Lachlan asked.

"Exactly."

Understanding dawned. "So we're going to ride you down?"

"That's the idea. I hope you're ready to hold your breath."

"Can we? For that long?" I asked. "How long will it take, by the way?"

"Not more than ten minutes."

"Yeah, that'll kill us," I said. Though, maybe not me, given my new ability to breathe water. Would that magic still work? I hoped so.

"I have something that will help," he said. "It won't be pleasant, but you'll get there. I wouldn't kill Jude's staff."

I had a feeling he'd do a lot more for Jude if she asked. I was dying to find out what was between them, but no way I could poke around there.

Shen led us through the street and out into the main part of the city. I assumed we were heading toward the river, and from the way Muffin was licking his chops, I had a feeling he was looking forward to it.

Why are these demons so afraid of missing out, anyway? he asked.

"What do you mean?"

FOMOrians. FOMO. You know. FOMO.

"What the heck is that?"

FOMO.

"Repeating it doesn't help."

He gave me a disgusted look. *You're really not hip with the youth, are you?*

"I think we've established that I'm not. And I don't think you are, either, if you say things like 'hip with the youth.'"

He hissed at me but continued speaking. *FOMO is Fear Of Missing Out. These Fomorians must have some real issues with FOMO.*

I laughed. "That's a terrible joke."

I kind of liked it.

"At least you're hip with the youth."

Exactly.

11

W e arrived at the edge of the river a few minutes later. It was in a more industrial part of town, with large barges pulled up to docks about a hundred yards down. We stopped in front of a chain-link fence.

I'll be back in a bit. Muffin crouched low and launched himself off the ground, little wings carrying him up and over the fence. He barely cleared it, but he managed. Maybe practice would help.

He flew over to the river, disappearing from sight.

"That's quite the familiar you have," Shen said.

"He's something else."

"He could have come this way." Shen pressed a hand to the fence, and magic flared on the air. "But I imagine he was excited about the river."

"He's always looking for tuna."

Shen gave the river a skeptical look. "I think he's going to be disappointed."

A door appeared, and we stepped through.

Shen led us to the edge of the river, where the water gleamed darkly under the moon. I shivered at the idea of what was down there.

Bodies. Definitely bodies.

I hadn't had much time for pop culture, but the mob and the big city always sprang to mind first for me.

Pretty morbid, really.

Shen turned to us. "I'll take you as far as the main gates. From there, you'll use your disguise to get in. You're traders, heading toward the market, and you're only there for a few hours." He dug into his pocket and handed me a small piece of silver attached to a chain. "When you need a ride back, press this. You can't transport out of there, so you'll have to wait for me. I'll be there within forty minutes. Maybe less. You'll be able to talk to me and get updates."

"Where will you pick us up? The drop-off point?"

"There's a tracking beacon on there. If you have to, you can depart their city anywhere, and I'll find you."

"Good." If we got in trouble while hunting The Three, we might need to bail quickly.

"Your contact will be Jonnie, a kid that you're most likely to find in the Daggered Heart, a bar that's popular with outsiders. He's got red hair and a tattoo of a bird on his neck."

"What language do they speak? Will we be able to find the bar, or will the sign be in Fomorian?"

"You'll recognize it, don't worry. I think it's at the back of town, far from the entrance." His gaze hardened. "Whatever you do, don't let them know you work for the Protectorate."

Lachlan nodded. "No problem."

Shen dug into his pocket and handed us each two tiny pills. "Take one of those. It'll help underwater."

I grinned. "Give us gills?"

"No, but it will keep you from dying. Take the other right before I pick you up."

I nodded, popping the pill in my mouth. I thought *maybe* I could breathe underwater. But now wasn't really the time to experiment. We needed to get this right. Warmth flowed through me as I swallowed the pill, a spark of magic that changed my body.

Shen's eyes widened. "Okay, you did that quick. Let's get moving."

As soon as he said the words, breathing became harder. Oops.

I struggled to gasp in a breath as Shen leapt into the water. As he splashed in, blue light bloomed around him, billowing out into the darkened river.

A second later, a dragon's head popped up. It had that distinctly Chinese look that was so different from European dragons. A broader head and brilliant emerald eyes, along with long whiskers. Sort of. I didn't know enough about Chinese dragon anatomy to guess what exactly they were called.

He was long, nearly thirty feet, and shaped more like a snake, with horn-like protrusions coming off his back.

With my lungs burning, I leapt into the river. The cold shocked a gasp from me, and as soon as I stuck my head in the water, I could breathe. It wasn't easy—more like sucking pudding into my lungs—but at least I could feel oxygen moving to my muscles.

Lachlan splashed in next to me, and we grabbed onto the dragon's back horns. I straddled him, with Lachlan a few feet behind me, and clung on.

Shen turned his head around, eyeing us with his gleaming emerald eyes. This close, his fangs glinted white. I really didn't want to get any closer to those giant chompers.

Then he plunged into the river. Cold enveloped me as he sped through the water.

At first it was dark. I couldn't make out anything beneath the

Hudson River. Which, given my preoccupation with mobsters and bodies, was fine by me.

The water seemed to race by at an unnatural speed. Faster than any kind of man-made submarine could go, at least.

By the time we made it out into the ocean, I could feel the difference. It felt cleaner down here, almost easier to breathe. Still pudding, but thin pudding.

And I realized that two massive beams of green light shot from Shen's face. His eyes, illuminating the water. The river must have been too full of mud and other crap for the light to cut through. Or he hadn't wanted humans spotting us. I had no idea.

But I liked the view of the ocean. It was pitch black anywhere that the light of his eyes didn't shine. But within the emerald gleam, I occasionally caught sight of a shark or a school of silver fish.

Normally, a shark might scare the crap out of me. But we were going so fast that the animals didn't stand a chance of catching us. I barely had a half second to even look at them before Shen dodged around.

As we cut through the ocean, deeper and deeper, my lungs began to burn. The pill was wearing off. Or it didn't like the depth.

Panic tugged at my mind briefly, but then my new magic seemed to kick in. Suddenly, breathing was a bit easier. As if Shen's charm wearing off had helped my own magic break through.

We needed to get there soon, though, because Lachlan didn't have this kind of helpful magic. Worry bloomed in my chest.

In the distance, I caught sight of a massive glowing dome.

Holy fates.

A city was built within, towers spiraling toward the top of the dome. Smaller domes were connected via little tunnels that made it possible to reach the annexes.

Was this what ancient scholars had meant by Atlantis? I had to assume so.

Shen slowed his approach as we neared one of the annexes. It was about the size of a large house, and inside, I could spot three guards.

Shen pulled to a stop at the edge of the annex, swimming right through an open spot in the water. A bubble of air. He made sure to keep his head out of the air, but the middle of his body, where we were sitting, was suddenly within the bubble.

I gasped, grateful for my first full breath. Beside me, Lachlan drew in a ragged breath. We climbed off of Shen, and he zipped away, disappearing into the water.

I looked up, awed. The dome itself wasn't made of plastic or glass, but rather magic. There was nothing between me and the ocean except this magical bubble. It made the air cool and humid, as if there was a ton of water mixed up with the oxygen.

"What's yer purpose?" a gravelly voice demanded.

Startled, I looked toward the other side of the bubble. There was a gate made of a strange white material—almost like bones. Whale bones?

I shivered and stepped toward the gate.

Three guards stood behind it, eyeing us suspiciously. The guards looked like fish demons of some sort, with green skin and gills at the sides of their necks. Their hair was made of seaweed, or something like it. They were probably perfect for this job, able to swim out and grab anyone who tried to take a water route.

Behind them, the tunnel stretched toward the main part of the city.

"We're here to trade energy stones at the market," Lachlan said.

Three pairs of brows rose at that.

"Energy stones?" demanded the gravel-voiced demon. "Those are rare."

"That's why we want to sell them." Lachlan grinned, and for the first time, it almost looked a little sleazy. He was trying to put on an act, I realized. He wasn't bad. "We'll get a pretty penny for something as rare as this."

He dug into his bag and grabbed something, then held up the only energy stone that was *actually* an energy stone. I had the other one in my pocket. It gleamed with a bright white light, and I couldn't help the covetous surge inside me. There was just something about these things that was so danged appealing.

Apparently, the guards agreed, because they opened the gate.

I stepped forward.

"Hold up!" Fish Man held up a hand, his face imperious. "Got to inspect the cargo."

Uh-oh.

There was a whole heck of a lot of greed on his face. More than he should have had, if he were just letting us through.

Nerves thrummed inside me. I shot Lachlan a glance as two of the three guards strode toward us. From the crease in his brow and the stiffness of his shoulders, I had to guess that Lachlan sensed the threat, too.

The gate slammed shut, leaving one guard behind, presumably with the button that would allow us entrance.

"Show us your cargo," Fish Man growled.

"He meant to say, *give* us your cargo," said the other guard.

Well, triple crap.

My gaze darted between the two guards who'd stopped in front of us, and the one who stood behind the gate. He had to press that button to let us through, so I couldn't kill him. And I couldn't alert him to our intentions by killing these guys either.

What the heck are we going to do?

"How about *one* stone?" Lachlan bargained.

"All of them."

If they got all of them, they'd realize we were frauds.

"Two stones," I said. "Our best ones."

"There is no best. There's just stones," said Fish Man. "And we want 'em all."

"Then we'll have nothing to trade and no way to pay our ride out of here," I said.

"Not our problem."

Crap. Okay, this was trouble.

My mind raced as my eyes darted all over the space. When they landed on Bojangles, who sat behind the guards who were hassling us, I almost gasped.

I bit it back.

The guard behind the gate couldn't see Bojangles where he sat.

Push the button! I begged with my mind, praying that Bojangles could hear me or understand me. Or at least interpret the situation for himself.

If this were Muffin, or even Princess Snowflake III, we'd have no trouble. But sweet Bojangles who chased his tail and maybe only had two brain cells to rub together?

I wasn't feeling super confident.

He grinned briefly, his white fangs glinting in the light, then his form shimmered and he disappeared. He was using his new invisibility power, I realized.

Was he doing what I'd asked?

"Well, hand it over!" Fish Man demanded.

Slowly, I began to remove my satchel, hoping to buy us a bit of time to see what Bojangles would do. Or if any of the other cats would show up.

Fish Man made a grabby-hands gesture, and I scowled. My heart thundered as I watched the guard behind the gate.

Suddenly, he shrieked, stumbling backward and slapping at his face. Red streaks appeared there.

Bojangles was attacking!

Lachlan and I leapt on the guards, taking them down to the ground.

Then time slowed. The guards stilled beneath us, frozen by Lachlan's magic.

"What now?" I asked.

"I don't think we should kill them," he said. "We're in their realm. They're technically demons. I don't know how the rules work here, but if we kill them, their souls might regenerate here."

"Good point." It was possible it wouldn't happen—the rules surrounding demons and their bodies were kinda weird sometimes—but we had to play it safe. "Bojangles! Don't kill him. Just incapacitate."

The little cat shrieked with malicious glee. He was probably mauling the hell out of the frozen demon.

"I'm going to unfreeze time," Lachlan said.

"Okay." I called a mallet from the ether. I rarely used this weapon, but on a whim, I'd imbued it with the spell that would keep it stored in my personal arsenal.

As time unfroze and the demon beneath me started struggling, I swung the mallet up, then smashed it into his head. Not enough to crush his skull, but he slumped to the side, unconscious. Lachlan did the same with his fist.

"Go get the other," he said. "He's probably nearly dead. I'll take care of these guys."

I scrambled to my feet and hurried to the gate. "Bojangles! Push the big button!"

I still couldn't see the cat, but the guard was a bloody mess on the floor. I winced at the sight of the deep scratches. Somehow, they looked even more painful than regular old sword wounds.

A moment later, the big button depressed. Bojangles appeared, sitting on top of it and grinning like mad. It was a slightly insane look, to be honest, but sweet in its own way.

The whale bone gate creaked open, and I rushed through.

"Did you kill him?"

Bojangles meowed, but I couldn't understand him. The guard looked unconscious, at the very least. His clothing was made of a rough brown leather-type material, and he had more strips of leather tied around his arms.

"Fish Man chic," I muttered as I yanked one of the arm bands off and tied it around his mouth. I did the same with two more bands, binding his arms and feet, then I stood and looked at Lachlan. "What are we going to do with them?"

"I've got a plan." He bent down and grabbed one Fish Man, swinging him over his shoulder. He did the same with another. "Be right back."

He stepped toward the edge of the dome, and his magic swelled on the air. The scent of evergreen with the taste of caramel on my tongue. He stopped at the edge of the dome, staring at the water. A moment later, it bowed inward, forming a space for him to walk into. The water kept pushing away from him, moving back and creating a fresh tunnel for him to walk through.

He got to an outcropping of rocks about twenty yards away and dropped the Fish Men there. One by one, he wedged them into a crevice in the rock, then he turned back and walked through the tunnel he'd made. The water closed in behind him, submerging the fish men, who were stuck between the rocks, unable to float away.

"Badass," I said as he appeared back in the tunnel. "I knew you could control water, but that's something else."

"It's one of my more powerful gifts. Someone will find them eventually. But with their gills, they should survive."

I looked down at my Fish Man, then out at the water. I wanted to try, too.

"I'm going to try," I said. "Will you help me drag him?"

While I could slowly drag one along the ground, we needed to move faster than that.

"Aye, I'll help. You've got new magic?"

"I think so."

Lachlan swept the Fish Man up into his arms as I stepped toward the wall of water behind me. I touched my fingertips to the tattoo of the torc around my neck, feeling it warm beneath my fingertips.

Slowly, I sucked in a breath and felt for the water around me, calling upon my magic in order to bend it to my will. Like a light switch turning on, I felt the water. *Felt* it, like I could feel my limbs.

A part of me.

I commanded the water to retreat, and it pressed backward, leaving an empty space for me to step into.

Wow.

Using my magic was so much easier than it had been. The torc really did help.

Victory, and a sense of accomplishment, flowed through me, making me grin. I walked along as the water parted for me, feeling like a magical Moses.

"Nicely done," Lachlan said from behind.

"Thanks. I can feel the difference in my magic. It's *amazing.*"

As soon as we reached the outcropping of rock, Lachlan stuffed the Fish Man in with his buddies, then we returned to the dome.

Bojangles was gone, no doubt off in search of something to eat.

"Your crew comes in handy," Lachlan said.

"I know. Lucky to have them." I started down the tunnel toward the main part of the city, my pace brisk. "We just need to disappear into the crowd before anyone finds the missing guards."

"Aye. Hopefully there will be more humans than just us."

12

As it turned out, there weren't more humans. Almost everyone that we saw when we reached the main part of town—the big bubble, as I liked to think of it—looked like a demon. Many of them had a fishy appearance, with gills and weeds for hair.

But some of them were more of the regular demonic variety. These were the bad guys of Celtic myth, and they looked it.

Fortunately, no one paid us too much attention as we walked down the street. There were a few glares, but otherwise, people ignored us. Apparently, they needed traders from the outside. Thank fates for Shen and his costumes.

Lachlan stuck close to my side as we passed buildings made of white stone that looked like bleached-out coral. Sea shells decorated some windowsills and doorways, but it didn't look cheery and beachy. Far from it.

Maybe it was the roofs, which dripped with dark seaweed. Insulation?

I had no idea.

The whole place was creepy, though. And the air felt way too wet to be comfortable.

"Shen said the Daggered Heart was on the other side of town, right?" I asked.

"Aye. We're getting close."

We passed a shop selling clamshells of all sizes, and another that specialized in pearls. There was a potions shop that looked like something out of The Vaults, and another that sold carriages pulled by giant seahorses. Or at least, that's what the sign said. I saw no trace of giant seahorses. The carriages were cool, though.

A man with a snail's shell for the back half of his body slimed past us, glaring and muttering, "Disgusting humans."

"He's one to talk." I turned around and checked out his slime trail, which gleamed behind him, then turned back to Lachlan. "This place is wild. No wonder Caro wanted to come."

"Aye, once in a lifetime."

"That'll be enough for me."

Something in the nearby shop window caught my eye. Muffin, sitting on a pile of fish. He had a skinny silver one chomped in his mouth and looked like he was in heaven. The shop owner was nowhere to be seen, and I didn't want to know what had happened to him.

"Muffin!" I hissed.

He turned to look at me, green eyes gleaming with excitement. He spat the fish out. *Come on in, the fish is great!*

"We have a job to do," I said.

He scowled. *I find paradise, and the first thing you want to do is drag me away? Buzzkill.*

I shook my head and kept walking. If I really needed help, I was confident that Muffin would show up. For now, I'd let him enjoy the fruits of his labor. Or murder. Or whatever it was he'd done to get that shop to himself.

"I think that's it." Lachlan pointed to a sign up ahead.

It hung off the door, protruding over the street. The thing

was made of wood and carved to look like a dagger stabbing straight into a heart.

"Yeah, let's hope Jonnie is here." I turned into the bar, immediately impressed.

It was done up like an old timey dance hall, or something like it. I didn't have enough experience with bars to say exactly what is was styled like, but there were cancan dancers on a stage at the back, their legs flying in the air beneath ruffly green skirts decorated with seaweed. They had fish heads, though, instead of human, and I kinda liked it.

The bar stretched along the wall to the left, and it was crowded with people. There were more humans in here than there had been out on the street, but they were still massively outnumbered by the Fomori. Tables full of demons played some kind of game with shells or watched the dancers while drinking green liquid that looked like sludge.

"Let's get a drink," Lachlan said. "Or at least stand near the bar so we don't stick out."

"Good plan."

We didn't have any Fomorian money, and I doubted they took cards down here, so we hovered at the bar behind a group of people waiting to order. They bought us some time to scout out our surroundings.

Lachlan faced the bar, trying to look like he was considering his options, while I turned to face him. I leaned against him casually, like we were just a couple, out for a nice date at a weird fish bar full of demons. But instead of looking at him, I peered around at the room behind him, trying to find Jonnie.

Most of the humans in here were women, which narrowed my options down. When I spotted a young guy sitting in the corner, scribbling into a notebook, my heart leapt.

"I think I see him."

"He got red hair?" Lachlan asked.

"Yep. And a tattoo of a bird on his neck."

"Bingo."

I stepped away from Lachlan, and he turned. Together, we walked toward Jonnie, who was obsessed with whatever he was writing in his notebook. He didn't even notice when we stopped at his table.

Or at least, I thought he didn't notice.

"Have a seat," he said without looking up.

He hadn't seen us, and we'd walked with silent footsteps, but somehow he'd noticed us. As I sat, he looked up, his eyes a piercing blue.

He squinted at me. "Who are you?"

Lachlan's magic swelled on the air, so faint I almost didn't recognize it. He was blocking the sound of our conversation, I thought. I glanced at him, and he nodded.

I turned to Jonnie. "I'm Ana Blackwood. You're Jonnie."

He nodded. "Yeah."

"Jude sent me."

His eyes flicked briefly. "Don't know any Jude."

"I'm from the Protectorate."

His face scrunched up in confusion. "No idea what you're talking about, mate."

He was deep undercover, and Jude had had no way to get him a message about our visit. And he'd left the Undercover Protectorate to come on this assignment before I'd ever showed up at the castle. My mind raced. I'd have to tell him something that made him believe me.

"My friend Lachlan here is blocking this conversation with his magic. No one can hear us. But Florian sends his regards. And the Pugs of Destruction." No one could know about Florian or the pugs unless they'd lived at the castle. "And Hans said he wishes you'd drink more juice. It's good for you."

Disbelief flashed on his face, then a small smile tugged at the corner of his mouth. "You a new member?"

I nodded. "Trainee. They let me out early for a special assignment."

"Something here, I gather?"

"Yes." I nodded my head toward Lachlan. "This is Lachlan Munro. He's helping me."

"I've heard of you. Potion genius, Mega Mage."

"Arch Magus," Lachlan said. "But I like Mega Mage better. Let's go with that."

Jonnie laughed and leaned back, closing his book. "What do you need here?"

"Help. I'm looking for three powerful figures who came here to hire an army. They're women, and they look like they're made of shadow. But they wear Roman armor."

"Like, ancient Roman?"

"Yeah."

"Weirdos." Jonnie shook his head. "Well, I can't tell you anything about the women, but there's only one place you want to go if you need an army. The Mercenary Guild."

"Where's that?"

"Edge of town, in its own annex near the theatre."

"How would we recognize it?" Lachlan asked.

"Oh, you'll recognize it. But you can't go alone. Won't stand a chance without me. It's hard for a human to pass here. I'll help you."

"Thanks." I smiled at him.

"No problem. I'm at a lull in my job anyway. Waiting for my own sources to come through. And if Jude let you out of training early for this, it must be important."

"Oh, it is." I shivered at the memory of what was happening to Otherworld. The Three might be gone, but their magic was probably still eating the land there, destroying it. And whatever they wanted their army for...I couldn't let them have it. No question.

"Can we go now?" Lachlan asked.

"Sure. This stuff is always a hurry, isn't it?" Jonnie said.

"Always."

We left the bar, following him out onto the street. It was still just as packed as ever, but Jonnie was adept at slipping through the crowd without drawing attention. He was like a ghost, the perfect undercover man.

We passed more strange shops and bars, along with houses that looked like something out of a creepy dream.

When we reached the theatre at the edge of town, I caught the sound of singing from inside, which was the most godawful racket I'd ever heard. Screeching and caterwauling like mad.

Jonnie glanced back at us. "Something, isn't it?"

"Sure is."

He stopped at the edge of town, where the dome pressed up against the sea. There was a tunnel leading outward, into the ocean.

"It's down there," Jonnie said.

"How do we break in?" Lachlan asked.

"We don't. Impossible. We'll have to be invited in. You got something to trade?"

"Yeah." I patted my bag. "Energy stones. How'd you know?"

"Shen's favorite disguise. I didn't think those silly hats were your choice. It works, too. Most of the time."

Hopefully *this* time.

"Give me a moment to change. I can't be recognized." He slipped into an alley that I hadn't noticed. There was a slight rustling sound, and he appeared a moment later, looking entirely different.

"You look like a demon." I eyed his bald head and horns, the yellow eyes and black fangs. "Why don't you stay like this the whole time you're in town here? They'd probably hassle you less."

"Can't hold it for that long. Transforming ain't easy, and the process isn't pretty. But if we're going to do something shady at the Mercenary Guild, I can't blow my cover."

"Fair enough. Thanks." I smiled at him.

"Let's go." He led the way down the tunnel, which narrowed as we reached the other end. "Let me do the talking, all right? Once we're in, we'll ambush the guard and go hunt down your answers. The code word is *kelp*."

"We attack on *kelp*?" I asked.

"Yep."

"No problem," Lachlan said.

The tunnel ended at an annex that was far bigger than the guard house we'd entered through. A freaking fortress fit within here, as big as the Protectorate castle and about eight hundred times creepier. It was built of bluntly carved black stone that was studded with barnacles. Seaweed dripped from the walls, gleaming with water and smelling like rotten vegetation. There were no windows that I could see.

A massive iron gate barred the front, dripping red with rust. The humidity in the air had to be killer on the iron.

"Why iron?" I asked. "Stainless steel would be so much better down here."

"Their main enemy are the fae," Jonnie said.

"Ah, right." Fae didn't like iron, from what I'd heard. Or it didn't like them. Either way, the two didn't mix.

"Wait here." Jonnie started toward the gate, and Lachlan and I obeyed.

"Oy! Guild!" Jonnie shouted. "Got some goodies for ya!"

About twenty feet up, one of the stones in the castle wall shifted. A figure peered out, green eyes blazing down at us. The guard was another Fish Man, but he was bulky with muscle. A massive sword glinted in his hand.

"What goodies?" he demanded.

"Energy stones. From some traders. Desperate traders."

I wanted to scowl, but it was actually a nice addition. They'd think they'd get a good price from us.

"*Real* energy stones?" Fish Man demanded.

Jonnie turned to us. "Hold up the goods."

Lachlan raised a hand, and the energy stone glowed bright within his fingertips.

Fish Man grunted and slammed the stone window shut. Then the iron gate began to creak, shrieking like a door that hadn't seen WD-40 in a decade. I almost had to cover my ears.

"Let's go," Jonnie said.

We followed him through the gate. Flecks of rust rained down on me, coating me in a weird red rain.

Four guards waited for us in the dark tunnel, their weapons raised high. Two had swords, while the other two held spears. Dark magic glowed around them, an inky black signature that I'd never seen before.

"Show us," the original Fish Man said.

I dug into my pocket and held out my one good energy stone, mimicking Lachlan. Tension thrummed in my muscles, waiting for the attack. What would I use? Weapons or magic?

My water power had worked. Did that mean I had flame and wind as well? Earth?

"That doesn't look like a lot," Fish Man said, shaking me from my thoughts.

"It's not." Jonnie grinned. "Now it's time for you to eat kelp."

Kelp.

I sprang into action as Jonnie sent a blast of blue magic hurtling toward them. It slammed into the Fish Man on the right, and he went rigid, his eyes rolling back into his head as he slammed to the ground.

I drew a dagger from the ether and hurled it, striking one of the Fish Men in the throat. Lachlan moved so fast I could hardly see him. He drew a sword and beheaded a Fish Man. Jonnie took out the fourth attacker, while I practiced my fire magic.

I envisioned shooting a bolt of flame. It felt natural as it shot from my hands, strong and bright.

Whoa.

I'd always bemoaned my defensive magic. Now I had offensive magic to spare.

"Nice." Lachlan grinned at me. "New power?"

"Yeah."

"We need to hide these bodies," Jonnie said. "It'll buy us a bit of time."

"Some demons wake up in their Underworld if you kill them, but do these guys?" The rules were a bit different since we were in their afterworld, but it wasn't technically the Underworld. Was it?

"Depends on the species. Most don't since we're on their home turf." He turned to look around. "Where the hell will we hide them?"

"I've got this." Lachlan's magic swelled on the air, and the ground in front of the demon bodies parted as he controlled the earth.

"Nice." Jonnie kicked a couple of the demons into the crack in the ground, and Lachlan finished off the rest. Then he closed up the earth.

I kicked some dirt over the crack, and it looked like nothing had ever happened.

I was going to have to try that sometime.

"Okay, let's see if we can find your targets," Jonnie said. "With any luck, they might still be here."

"Maybe." I sniffed, trying to get a whiff of their distinctive magical signature, but came up blank. It was too hard to tell in a place that stank as badly as this one did. "Can't tell."

"You said you wanted to know if The Three got an army, right?" Jonnie asked.

"Yeah."

"Let's go check the armory, then. And the merc quarters."

"You know where those are?" Lachlan asked.

"Yeah. I've been in here a time or two looking for info. They haven't let me get off the ground floor, but there's a lot to be seen and learned down here. Fortunately for you, this is where the mercs hang out."

"We'll start with that, then." We needed as much info as we could get before we were caught. This felt like playing it smart and safe.

"This way." Jonnie led us through the tunnel, stopping at the point where it spilled out into an open courtyard.

Fortunately, the space wasn't wide, so we wouldn't have to cross much open terrain. On the other side, the enormous fortress soared high above us. The whole thing was made of huge black stones, and every angle was sharp. It was a villain's castle if I'd ever seen one, meant to threaten and intimidate. Even the light was darker here. And above, the black ocean loomed.

Jonnie peered up, squinting toward what I assumed were guard posts set into the exterior curtain wall.

"I don't see anyone," he said.

"Hang on, I'll slow time," Lachlan said.

Jonnie looked at him with a hint of respect in his eyes. "All right, mate. You do that. I like traveling with you."

Lachlan's magic swelled briefly on the air, so faint I almost didn't sense it. Had I not been searching for it, I never would have. Then the air got that distinctive heavy feeling.

"Let's go," Lachlan said. "I can't hold it long."

We hurried across the courtyard, darting into another tunnel that cut beneath the huge fortress. Once we were out of sight of the guards, Lachlan dropped the time-slowing spell.

We followed Jonnie on silent feet, creeping through the tunnels toward the back of the compound. He made a right, then a left, and finally, we were at a massive set of iron doors.

Jonnie sighed and turned to us. "Bad news, friends. Armory is empty."

"How do you know?"

"No guards at the doors." He turned to them and pushed one open.

I peeked my head inside, and damned if he wasn't right. There were thousands of empty spots along the walls where swords and other weapons would have once hung. Not a single one remained.

Disappointment tightened around my heart like a steel vise. I turned to Jonnie and Lachlan. "That means they've already left. The Three got their army."

"But where are they headed?" Lachlan asked.

That was the million dollar question.

13

"They can't be far ahead of us," Lachlan said.

"Whatever they offered the Mercenary Guild had to be compelling. Getting their whole army like that..." Jonnie shook his head, clearly impressed.

"Is it big?" I asked.

"Over a hundred. Maybe a lot over a hundred. And all highly trained mercs. Mostly Fomori, but other demons as well."

"We need to find out where they've gone," Lachlan said.

"Let's head to the mercenary quarters," Jonnie said. "It's not far from here, and maybe there are some stragglers who haven't headed out yet."

We left the armory behind and continued our silent progress through the fortress. It was quiet, which wasn't a surprise if most of the army was already off getting ready for battle.

As we walked, I pressed my fingertips to the comms charm at my neck. "Bree? Rowan?"

"Hey, how's it going?" Bree answered.

"The Three have their army. They've left. I think you should tell Jude so she can gather forces. We'll need to stop them."

"Know where they went?"

"Trying to figure that out now."

"Good luck."

"Thanks," I said.

"And be safe."

"You too." I cut the connection.

By the time we reached the mercenary quarters, my heart was thundering. I needed answers like I needed air. We'd always been one step behind The Three, and eventually, that was going to turn deadly.

Jonnie led us into an empty hallway built of rough black stone. The floor beneath was made of more rock, and it felt like walking inside a huge mountain.

"I've never been this far," Jonnie whispered. "But this is where they live."

We passed room after room, all of the doors closed. Dormitories?

My skin prickled as we walked, tension racing up and down my arms as I waited for something to happen. My druid sense didn't pull me toward any doors, so I didn't open them, but I felt that there was knowledge here. Somewhere.

Frustration welled within me as we kept walking. I couldn't stay one step behind them the whole time. We'd never catch up.

When a demon stepped into the hall in front of us, I leapt into action. This was the moment I'd been waiting for.

I called upon my magic, using the torc as a conduit. The power surged within me, lighting up my chest with energy. I envisioned sending a blast of air at the demon, throwing out my arms so that my palms faced him. It worked.

Wind howled from my palms, shooting down the corridor and bowling the demon over. He flipped head over heels as he tumbled down the hall.

"Whoa," Jonnie muttered.

I raced after the demon, sprinting until I reached him. He lay on his back, stunned and staring up at the ceiling.

I straddled him and drew a dagger from the ether, then pushed it to his throat. He had pale yellow skin with a green tinge underneath, and his large horns were black. The magic that rolled off him stank of rot and decay.

I shuddered.

"I'll kill you. Happily." I gave him a grin that I knew looked insane. It probably helped my cause, actually. "Tell me where the rest of the mercenaries went."

"I can't, I'll—"

I pressed the blade against his throat until a bead of blood welled. "Tell me."

"I don't know!"

I pressed the blade deeper.

"I don't know! They didn't tell me."

I scowled, believing him.

"Where would I find information?"

His acid green eyes widened and darted, clearly searching for help. But he could see only Lachlan and Jonnie, and I'd bet they didn't look very helpful right now.

I pressed the dagger a little deeper, wondering how much farther I could go before it was lights out. "Tell me."

"The war room! They plan all attacks in the war room. You'll probably find something there."

"Where is it?"

"Back of the castle, up the tower. But it's impossible to get to without an invitation."

"How do we know which tower?"

"You'll know. It's the worst place you've ever been in your life."

He looked so sure that I believed him. "How many soldiers left here?"

"About a hundred. Maybe more."

So, confirming what Jonnie had said. That was a lot, considering they were all highly trained mercs. No matter where they were going, we were definitely going to need backup to deal with them.

I stared down at the demon, debating. I could kill him. I *should* kill him. Magical signatures didn't lie. He was evil. But I was in the position of power here. It would make me an executioner, and I didn't want that. I preferred an even fight where my life was at stake.

That wasn't the case here. And this...this wasn't me.

Normally, you knew that if you killed a demon on earth, he'd end up back in the underworld, where he belonged. It wasn't killing so much as it was banishing him back to the place where he could do no harm.

But this...

I didn't know if he'd wake up in the underworld, or if this was his original realm. If I killed him, it could be permanent. For good.

No thanks.

I hit him on the head with the butt of my dagger, and he passed out. Quickly, I bound his mouth and limbs, then looked up at Lachlan. "Shove him in a room, will you?"

He picked up the unconscious demon like he weighed nothing and put him in the nearest room. I stood, brushing off my hands, and looked at them. "Ready?"

"Aye," Lachlan said.

Jonnie nodded.

We headed off through the castle again. It was silent still. The sound of footsteps in one hall made us dart into an alcove and wait it out, but we continued without issue. Toward the back of the castle, the air began to grow colder. Icy. Misery seeped into my veins.

Dread opened a hole in my chest. "We're almost there."

"How can you tell?" Jonnie rubbed his chest, a sickly green color tinging his skin.

"Phantoms." I shuddered. "Demon said that the tower was the worst place in the world. Well, that means Phantoms."

"They must guard it," Lachlan said.

"That's my thought." I nodded. "So we just have to get through them."

"How?" Jonnie asked.

The options were shit. "Think happy thoughts. Try not to touch them. And run."

Jonnie grimaced. "That's it?"

"Unfortunately, yeah. But I've done it before, and I'll do it again. You'll be fine. Just keep a stiff upper lip, and we'll make it through."

He nodded, determination setting his brow. He looked so much like a demon that it was weird to be working with him, but I could still see the real him beneath it all.

We continued on, toward the icy cold and misery.

By the time we reached the Phantoms, my hands were shaking. I hated this part.

They lined a hallway that terminated at an empty space where a door should be. It was pitch black within the doorway, and somehow, that was worse. There were at least twenty Phantoms standing along the wall. A constant guard.

No one in their right mind would walk through that gauntlet. It probably wasn't even possible. Sometimes Phantoms would reach out to touch you, sometimes not. Either way, it was beyond miserable.

I sucked in a breath and looked at my companions. "Ready?"

They nodded.

"Remember, happy thoughts." I started forward, dredging up memories of playing with my sisters when we were young. In the rare moments that we forgot we were hunted. As teenagers, finishing a job in Death Valley and counting our money. Before we handed it over to the mobster, of course.

As I neared the Phantoms, the air grew even colder. I could have been standing on Everest, it was so chilly. My skin prickled and my veins flooded with ice.

Agony speared me as I reached the first Phantom, stabbing through my brain. I sprinted forward, trying to get it over with, but they were so powerful that my limbs slowed.

Visions of my sisters, dead, flashed through my mind.

The memory of my mother's death.

Realizing that Rowan was missing, afraid for the worst.

Lachlan being killed.

All of my greatest fears and worst memories flashed through my mind. The Phantoms reached out with transparent blue claws, swiping at my arms. Pain sliced through me wherever they touched me, drawing a ragged gasp from my throat.

I stumbled, nearly going to my knees, but Lachlan dragged me up by the arm. I clung to him, and we kept going, staggering past the Phantoms.

Turn back, a voice hissed inside my head. *Turn back or it will all come true.*

Panic flared in my chest, a grasping thing that squeezed at my heart.

Was it true?

Could all of these horrible visions come true if I kept going?

No.

That was the craziness of fear talking. I wouldn't believe it. I couldn't.

I *had* to keep going. *Had to.*

Three times, I almost turned back. The Phantoms were so compelling. I believed them—almost. If I kept going, my sisters and everything I loved would be gone. All of my worst fears would come true.

By the time I passed them, I was sweaty and my eyes were wet with tears. Panting, I stumbled to a stop inside the dark room that was at the end of the hall. With shaking muscles, I leaned against the cold stone wall and gasped.

"Are you all right?" Lachlan's voice was rough.

"Yeah." I ran a trembling hand over my face. "You?"

"Fine." He looked at Jonnie, who was white as a sheet. "Jonnie?"

"Peachy."

I chuckled, but it was a weak sound. It took a few minutes for the worst of the fear to subside. I'd never had it that bad with Phantoms before. These ones had been extra powerful, with the added jolt of being able to make me believe it would all come true.

But my fears had changed, hadn't they?

I'd always been afraid for my family and friends, but now, that was *all* I'd been afraid of. In the past, there'd always been a smattering of fear that I'd never get my magic. That I'd never be good enough.

But I had my magic.

I was worthy.

And, it turned out, I kind of believed it.

I grinned. That was pretty dang awesome.

"We're in the tower." Lachlan's voice shook me from my thoughts.

I blinked and looked upward, following his gaze.

He was right. The room was circular and tall, extending up at least fifty feet, probably more. But there were no stairs. Just an empty column that led to a room at the top. At least, I assumed there was a room at the top.

My druid sense seemed to like the idea of me trying to get up there, at least. It pulled toward the top of the tower.

"There's got to be a way up," I said.

Jonnie and Lachlan started searching the walls, and I joined them. I raised my hand, igniting the lightstone ring, and squinted through the gloom.

Near the entrance, there was a fancy inscribed symbol. Like something you would press a spy ring to and it would match the symbol and make stairs appear, or something.

Unfortunately, we had nothing that looked like that.

Jonnie appeared at my shoulder, squinting at the little carved inscription. "I can try to make a match."

"Conjurer?" Lachlan asked.

"Yep." Magic glowed around his hands, smelling something like a new car. Strange signature, but not bad. A moment later, a little iron ring appeared in his hands. He pressed it to the inscribed symbol in the wall and said, "No guarantees."

I waited, breath held, but nothing happened.

Jonnie's shoulders drooped. "Dang. Needs some magic."

"Like something to trigger the spell?" I asked.

"Exactly. Prevents something like this from happening."

"Thanks for trying." I leaned back and inspected the walls again. No way I was giving up.

After a few moments of inspection, I realized that the stones that made up the interior of the tower wall were so rough they created handholds every few feet. Some were really tiny, but they would do the job.

"It might be possible to climb this thing." I shivered as I said the words.

Lachlan gave me a look, and I shrugged. "Got no choice."

I might be scared, but if this was the only way, I was headed up, no matter how I had to get there.

I picked a particularly large set of grooves in the wall and started climbing. My fingers ached as I ascended, and my heart thundered like a freaking drum line. There was a marching band in my chest, and they were playing some scary freaking music.

Lachlan and Jonnie joined me, picking their own routes up the tower. Smart. Lachlan eventually lined up below me, with Jonnie to the right.

"Might not want to be under me," I muttered. "In case I take a dive."

"I've got you," Lachlan said.

What, he planned to catch me with one arm while climbing up a wall like a hulking Spiderman? Actually, I wouldn't put it past him.

That slowed my heart a bit, and I kept climbing, hand over hand.

My fingertips slipped on a particularly narrow crevice, and my stomach almost lodged itself in my throat. I scrambled for a handhold and made it, pressing myself against the wall and panting.

Holy fates, this was too much.

Muffin appeared beside me, fluttering in the air on his little wings. *You look like you've swallowed rotten tuna.*

I stifled a laugh and pressed my cheek to the stone, panting. "That's not helping."

Just saying. I calls it like I sees it.

I ignored him and kept climbing. We were halfway up when Muffin screeched. *Shield! Incoming from above!*

Instinct drove me as my magic kicked into action. I dredged up my shield power, the original magic that I'd had all my life. I didn't know what was coming, but I trusted Muffin.

The magic struggled slightly, but finally, it burst to life, creating a shield over me, Lachlan, and Jonnie. Muffin hovered beside me, little wrinkled face turned upward.

When the acid splashed onto the shield, my magic faltered. I sucked in a deep breath and pushed myself hard, imagining a strong and impenetrable shield. This magic was now the hardest for me to use, since it wasn't a gift of the gods. Bree had lost her root power when she'd transitioned to Dragon God.

Would I?

I *really* didn't want to. For all that I'd complained about having defensive magic in an offensive world, it was really danged handy.

My fingertips ached as I clung to the wall and looked up. Green acid—either magic or the real thing—was pouring from above. Some kind of repellent charm meant to stop invaders. They should have sanded down the sides of the walls, but apparently this had been easier.

They hadn't expected someone like me to break in.

"Can you hold your shield?" Lachlan asked.

"I think so." My voice was shaky and weak as I gave every ounce of strength that I had to the magic. "Keep going."

The acid battered at my shield as we climbed, pouring over the edge and raining down in the middle of the empty tower. If we fell, we'd be smashed on the stones below, then covered in acid.

Hell no.

You're doing great!

Muffin sounded like a kindergarten teacher, full of cheer and encouragement. It felt a bit strange considering the circumstances, but I didn't have the energy to call him out on it.

Keep going! Almost there!

I expected him to be waving little pom-poms in his front paws, but I didn't spare him a look.

Every muscle ached as we climbed, and my magic was really starting to falter by the time we neared the top. I was running out. Then I felt a prickle of magic that signaled *this* was where the acid spell had begun. As soon as we passed it, the stuff stopped coming.

Panting, I clung to the wall and tried to catch my breath.

"I see a trapdoor to the right," Lachlan said.

His fingertips scraped against stone as he climbed that way. Jonnie followed. I watched as Lachlan tugged at the door. It didn't budge.

Crap.

Then his magic swelled on the air, bringing with it the fresh scent of pine and the taste of caramel on my tongue. Lachlan pressed his fingertips to the iron ring that was sunk into the door. It glowed bright red, then began to melt, droplets falling to the ground below. When enough of the iron latch had melted, the wooden door swung open.

Quick as a flash, Lachlan climbed up into the tower above.

"All good." His voice echoed down.

Jonnie followed, and I trailed after. Lachlan helped pull me up into the room above, and honestly, I wasn't going to complain. Fear had turned my muscles to jelly.

Somehow, I'd managed to spend all my life on flat ground. But lately, I'd had to climb so many insanely tall things that it was ridiculous.

"Nicely done," Jonnie said. "We'd have been toast without your shield."

I nodded, grateful it had kept working. It was harder to use and weaker than it had once been—a result of my body filling up with other magic and pushing out my original power—but at least it had worked. I vowed to practice it constantly so I didn't lose it. We needed it too much.

On trembling legs, I turned and inspected the room. It was empty, thank fates, the leaders no doubt having gone along with the army. The walls were lined with bookshelves that were stuffed full of books and scrolls. In the middle, there was a large table.

I approached it, squinting at the three-dimensional model set up there. It was a battle plan, clearly, showing a village and a horde of demons approaching from the side, ready to attack.

I blinked, shocked.

The village was on a hill, and it had three walls surrounding it. My skin turned to ice.

My mother's village.

14

"It's my mother's village," I whispered.

"Where?" Jonnie asked.

"Celtic Otherworld."

Lachlan pulled a cell phone from his pocket and snapped a picture right before Muffin sat down and swiped at the battle plan with his tail, destroying the setup.

In the upper left corner of the campaign board, there was writing. In Latin?

I pointed to it. "Can anyone read that?"

Jonnie leaned over and squinted. "Campaign of The Fates. In Latin."

I blinked. The Fates?

I looked at Lachlan. "Do you think they're really the three fates? Like, the famous ones?"

"They could be," Lachlan said.

"But they control the thread of human life. One snip, and you're done. They could have killed us already."

"Maybe they can't," Jonnie said. "Maybe they've lost their power."

Could be. Either way, we had to get a move on. Whatever

their motive, there was no time to waste. "We've got to get out of here. The village will need backup."

I pressed my fingertips to my comms charm and ignited the magic. When Rowan picked up, I told her what I'd learned.

"Just get back here. We'll be ready," she said.

"On it."

I made a second call to Shen, letting him know we'd need a pick-up real soon.

"Be there in thirty."

"Hurry." I swallowed hard, hoping he'd make it in time.

"This way," Jonnie said from beside a door to the left. Apparently, the top of the tower was joined to other parts of the castle.

Would the ground floor even be accessible from this level, or would we have to climb back down the tower?

It was worth exploring other options, that was for sure.

As soon as we stepped through the door, an alarm rang out. It tore through my head.

"Intruder alert." Lachlan's voice was grim.

"Let's go!" I sprinted down the hall. We couldn't get stuck here. The Protectorate needed the details of the attack.

The passage was dark and narrow, built of the same rough black stone as the tower. When demons appeared in front of us, having run from another adjoining hall, I didn't hesitate.

They loomed in front of us, at least twelve of them, all armed to the gills. They looked like a cross between sea monsters and demons. More Fish Men, but even more evil-looking. Their dark green skin was covered in barnacles, and their horns looked like they were made of black shell. Blazing green eyes gleamed with murder. They roared and raised their weapons.

I called upon my new fire magic, wondering which god had given this to me. The power ripped through me. I threw out my arms, and flames burst forth, roaring through the hall and plowing into the demons.

Shrieks filled the air as five of them fell, engulfed in flame. There were still about ten behind them.

Jonnie lunged in front of me, hurling a blast of his blue light magic. It slammed into half of them, and they stiffened. Their eyes rolled back into their heads, and they slammed to the ground.

There were four left.

Two of them threw long daggers. I was too slow with my shield, so we dived out of the way. A dagger sliced across my shoulder. Pain flared, but years of experience told me that the cut was shallow.

I drew my own dagger from the ether and stumbled to my feet.

To my left, a flash of magic revealed Lachlan in his black lion form. He roared and charged, his midnight fur gleaming in the light. He was so big that he took up nearly the entire hall.

I clutched my dagger and lowered it to my side. "No point in throwing now that he's out there."

"Truth," Jonnie said.

Lachlan tore through the rest of the demons, a green liquid flying as he went to town with fangs and claws.

Muffin fluttered next to me. *I don't think those Fish Men would taste very good.*

"Nope." I grimaced as a green arm flew toward us. "The neon blood is really off-putting."

And they stink of rotten seaweed. I don't like salad. Especially not rotten salad.

Lachlan finished in record time, then shifted back. We joined him, leaping over the dismembered demons and continuing on. The alarm continued to sound, pounding through my head and making my brain hurt.

Twenty yards later, the hallway abruptly stopped. A metal door blocked our way.

I stepped back and looked at Lachlan. "Work your magic."

He grinned and pressed his hand to the metal. Tension thrummed across my skin as I waited for the door to heat. I stepped back, giving him room, and Jonnie followed. It glowed red and began to sag, then in a whoosh, the metal dropped, molten and puddling on the floor.

Lachlan leapt over it.

"Nice." I took a running start and jumped over the metal.

We continued on, sprinting down the hall and looking for any kind of exit.

When the stone building began to tremble, my breath caught.

Oh crap.

Something bad was coming.

Right in front of us, the hallway broke apart. Light shined in as the hall began to swing.

"How the hell is that happening?" Jonnie asked.

"Crazy magic." The ground beneath me shifted as the hallway swung left, revealing nothing but open sky. Finally, the hall stopped rotating. About twenty feet away, I could see the top of the exterior castle wall. At least, that's what I thought it was.

I crept forward on trembling legs, hoping the ground wouldn't give out beneath me. What I saw at the end made me gasp.

The hallway had swung out so that it now hovered over the open courtyard, which was about a hundred feet below. My stomach pitched as I stared down at the demons.

They roared, apparently having caught sight of my face. One threw a fireball at me. The orange flame hurtled upward, and I lunged back, desperate to avoid it.

Lachlan caught me.

Jonnie crept to the edge and peered over, then lunged backward. An orange fireball flew through the air a moment later.

He turned to us. "I have a plan."

"Good, because I got nothing." I was still shaking from the horrible view downward.

"Can you make your shield again?" he asked.

"I think so."

"You need to know so."

A memory of it faltering against the Kobolds flashed through my mind, but I ignored it. "I'm pretty sure."

Jonnie frowned. "Good enough."

"It's the best we're getting."

He grinned. "Excellent, then."

He explained his plan, and I wanted to vomit. Lachlan looked leery as well, but it was our only option. We both agreed.

Jonnie edged up to where the hallway broke off and looked back at us. "Okay, get ready."

Lachlan and I both nodded.

Jonnie's magic flared on the air, that strange new car smell, and a heavy wooden board appeared in front of him. It was twenty feet long and two wide.

Lachlan joined him, and they pushed it out across open space until it caught on the top of the exterior curtain wall twenty feet away.

Jonnie pointed to Lachlan. "You're up, man."

Lachlan stepped toward the edge and raised his hands. His magic filled the air, and briefly, time stopped. Silence descended and the demons below froze.

"Nice." Jonnie grinned.

Then the spell broke. Fireballs flashed upward. We lunged back.

"Crap! What happened?" I asked.

Lachlan crept toward the edge and peered over, then cursed. "They've got a time manipulator too. He blocked my spell."

"Aw, hell," Jonnie muttered.

"I can shield us as we cross," I said. "But it's going to be iffy."

"It'll have to do," Lachlan said. "I'll keep their time manipulator from freezing us."

I sucked in a deep breath and called on my shield magic, getting ready to protect the bridge and us.

"Let's go!" Jonnie darted out onto the bridge, and I followed, Lachlan bringing up the rear.

I put all my attention toward the shield that protected us from below. It had the added benefit of making sure I didn't focus on the demons who were trying to blow us away. Red light flashed at the bottom edge of my vision, no doubt fireballs slamming into my shield. I could feel every single one like a physical blow.

"You're doing great," Lachlan said.

I kept my gaze on the board and the wall ahead as I walked, forcing my magic to keep the shield alive.

It began to falter as I neared the other wall. One of the fireballs blasted up past my shoulder, the heat searing me.

"Hurry!" I shouted.

Jonnie picked up the pace, and I followed, desperately trying to keep my footing and the shield in their proper positions.

Another fireball broke through, this one nearly plowing into Jonnie. It missed our bridge by inches, thank fates.

A moment later, Jonnie leapt onto the top of the stone wall, scrambling to safety. My shield was really faltering by the time I reached the wall, the repeated blows having damaged it.

Jonnie reached for me and dragged me over. The wall was about fifteen feet wide, a massive structure that had to be almost impenetrable. It was crenellated, with those big square protrusions that were common on medieval castles and provided great cover for guards and archers.

I turned just in time to see a fireball slam directly into the back end of our bridge, the part that was so far away it wasn't protected by my shield. The wood splintered and Lachlan wobbled.

A millisecond later, the bridge flipped, disappearing out from under him.

Fear stabbed me in the chest as he lunged, reaching for the stone wall. His fingertips grabbed it, and he clung on. Panicked, I knelt to help him up, but he'd already heaved himself onto the wall.

"Holy fates, that was close," Jonnie said.

"I'm so sorry." I pulled Lachlan up, though he didn't really need my help.

"Not a problem." He grinned at me, pressing a quick kiss to my forehead. "We're all here."

"Phase two." Jonnie stepped back and raised his arms, magic flaring on the air.

Huge coiled ropes appeared at his feet, and Lachlan got to work tying them off to the crenellations.

"So, you don't like heights?" Jonnie asked.

"Nope. About as much as I like taxes." Which I'd never paid since I'd always lived off the grid.

"Could have fooled me." Jonnie bent and grabbed a rope. "Good luck, and try to be quick."

I grabbed my own rope, and Lachlan did the same. We stood at the edge, our backs to the wind, and I looked at him.

"You've got this," he said.

"I do." After the Eiffel Tower, the freaking beanstalk, and finally, the damned devil climb we'd just done, I was a freaking pro.

I dropped off the edge, rappelling down as fast as I could.

Muffin kept pace with me. *You're doing great! I'll catch you if you fall!*

Ha. As if. My weight would take us both down.

I ignored the thought and focused on the climb, determined

to make this happen. By the time I felt solid ground beneath my feet, sweat was dripping in sticky lines down my back.

Jonnie turned to us. "We've got to split up from here. I can't be caught. You good?"

"We're good," I said. "Thanks for the help."

"And good luck on your mission," Lachlan said.

Jonnie saluted and ran off, headed who knew where. I turned to Lachlan. "Let's get the hell out of here."

We sprinted along the edge of castle wall, headed back toward the tunnel that led to the main part of the city. We had to get out of this annex before the guards spotted us.

Unfortunately, things never worked that easily.

By the time we reached the tunnel, more guards had spilled out of the castle entrance.

"Where the hell were they hiding?" I panted. It'd been easy to sneak in, but getting out was hell.

In a flash of light, Lachlan shifted into his black lion form. I leapt onto his back, and he thundered down the tunnel, huge paws eating up the ground. If we could just make it into the main part of the city, maybe we could get lost until Shen came to pick us up.

We were halfway there when another army appeared, right in front of us. More mercenaries. At least twenty of them.

Shit.

We were blocked on both sides, trapped in this tunnel with millions of pounds of water all around.

The Cats of Catastrophe appeared, which only affirmed that we were screwed. They only came when crap really hit the fan.

Princess Snowflake III galloped toward one of the oncoming mercs, her white fur blowing in the wind. She'd look a bit ridiculous as a defender if I didn't know what she was capable of. But even I didn't expect what came next.

She stopped and opened her mouth, shooting a blast of

flame that was so big it filled the cavern, immolating the oncoming demons.

"Holy fates," Lachlan said. "She learned a new trick."

Boy, had she. The fire was too great for us to even pass through, so that way was cut off.

The demons coming from the other end began to shriek, chaos erupting amongst themselves. Red slashes appeared across their faces and chest, so fast that it looked like an invisible lawnmower had gotten to them.

Bojangles.

Damn, that cat was mean when he wasn't chasing butterflies.

Muffin hovered near my head, wrinkled face close to mine. *There's more coming. The city got the intruder alert. You can't go that way.*

Crap. I relayed the message to Lachlan.

He frowned. "We've got to go out into the sea."

"How long could our air bubbles hold?" We could make our own passages, but we couldn't make oxygen. We'd eventually breathe it all up.

"I don't think it matters. We have to risk it."

Princess Snowflake III's flame was starting to falter, and Bojangles's demons were beginning to calm down a bit. We were losing our advantage.

"Yep, do it." The charm that Shen had given me had a tracking beacon on it, so he should be able to find us. "Shen should be here soon. We'll make it."

Lachlan stepped up to the edge of the tunnel, his magic filling the air. The water bowed outward as he forced it back. I followed him into the new tunnel he'd created.

"I'll do what I can, then you take over," he said.

We pushed our way through the water, Lachlan building more and more tunnel as we walked, forcing the water away from us.

Muffin hissed. *Incoming!*

I turned, catching sight of demons spilling into our new tunnel. "Cut them off!"

Lachlan glanced back. A second later, water splashed in on the demons.

Our tunnel was cut off from its air source. We were officially in our own little bubble, deep under the Atlantic Ocean.

"How long do you think we have?" My breath heaved, sucking up as much oxygen as possible. I forced myself to slow. We couldn't afford for me to freak out right now. Totally not an option.

"No idea," Lachlan said.

We made our way across the seafloor, putting as much distance as we could between us and the demons who pursued us. The ground beneath my feet was a combo of mud and sand, and we passed coral heads that were larger than I was.

I turned to check our progress and caught sight of the Fish Men swimming toward us, spears in their hands. "Oh crap. They're coming."

And *that* was the major downside of not having gills and flippers. I might've been able to breathe underwater, but I was still as awkward as a human. I didn't stand a chance.

Lachlan still had enough power to keep commanding the water to move out of the way of our air bubble, but I added my power to his. We needed to move faster.

This was like the slowest, weirdest chase in the history of magic. At one point, a giant grouper stared at us with his huge eyes.

Too bad you aren't a fishy Snow White, Muffin meowed. *You could tell that big tasty fish to attack the demons.*

That *would* be convenient.

But I couldn't, and the demons were so damned close. Their

bright green eyes glowed through the dark as they neared. I drew my sword from the ether, ready for them.

"They're coming," I said. "You keep the bubble going. I'll fight."

Muffin meowed. *Fish Men for dinner!*

When the first one broke through our barrier, I lunged, stabbing with my sword. I pierced him through his gilled throat, then kicked him in the stomach and forced him back into the water.

The trauma to the edge of the bubble caused air to flutter away from our main compartment.

Oh no.

Every attack would make our bubble smaller. And was the air already getting harder to breathe?

I shook away the worry and focused on the next Fish Man. He burst through, followed by a partner that I hadn't noticed. I went for the first guy. Muffin went for the second.

I swiped my sword across his chest as he jabbed out with his spear. I dodged the spear, and green blood poured from the wound. He roared.

Muffin attacked the other, claws flying as he flew around the Fish Man's head.

I kicked my wounded Fish Man out of our bubble, then did the same with Muffin's.

We could do this!

We just had to hold them off until Shen got here. Not much longer.

Right?

We kept moving and fighting, moving and fighting.

Then the attack came. A dozen of them. Reinforcements, maybe. Their eyes glowed in the ocean as they neared.

"Take Shen's pill!" I shouted. "Incoming!"

I dug into my pocket and shoved the pill into my mouth,

then swallowed quickly. It would help me breathe. For a little while, at least. My heart thundered as they neared.

"You better scram, Muffin." My voice trembled.

I was afraid of heights, but also apparently of drowning thousands of feet below the ocean's surface.

Muffin disappeared, thank fates.

The Fish Men attacked as one, surrounding the bubble and plowing inside. Such a huge attack broke the surface tension that kept the bubble in shape.

The world exploded around me as our huge bubble turned into thousands of small ones that shot to the surface of the ocean, leaving us behind.

Suddenly, I was slow and awkward, kicking and swinging my sword at the attacking Fish Men. They were graceful and agile, used to this strange world. I tried to control the ocean, but water rushing against water didn't mean much. It had to interact with something, like air, for me to have any effect.

From the corner of my eye, I caught sight of Lachlan.

Somehow, he fought with grace and power, wounding any Fish Man that approached. But they were too fast and too strong. Too many of them.

I couldn't create fire down here, nor wind, but I tried the earth, making the sandy bottom rise up and slam into the Fish Men that attacked. It wasn't perfect—I was too slow underwater—but it held them off as I tried to kick my way to the surface, Lachlan at my side.

But we were too far down. It'd take hours at this speed. We barely had ten minutes.

We were screwed.

15

Panic started to tighten like a vise around my muscles. When I caught sight of the bright green lights cutting through the ocean, elation filled me.

"Shen!" I tried to scream.

But just bubbles came out.

He seemed to hear a hint of noise, though, and turned toward us, cutting through the water with killer efficiency. He opened his massive mouth and roared, the sound vibrating the water around us.

The Fish Men panicked, swimming away from us as fast as they could. Shen swam by, and we grabbed on, clinging to the spikes that protruded from his back.

To the surface! I tried to scream at him. None of that diagonal long way. Straight to the surface of the river in Manhattan. I needed to get some freaking air. Lachlan, even more so. He didn't have my ability to breathe underwater.

There was no way Shen could have heard us, but he wasn't an idiot. He'd seen our situation when he arrived.

The sea dragon shot for the surface, swimming straight up.

The water tore at my hair as we ascended, and I clung to him. No freaking way I'd be losing my grip now.

When we broke through the surface, I sucked in a happy breath. Oh fates, that felt good.

Waves lapped at us as I gasped raggedly. A huge moon gleamed on the ocean. There was nothing for miles. Not a speck of land or a single ship. The air was cool and the ocean colder.

I collapsed on Shen. "Definitely a one-time thing."

"Aye, I've seen enough of the realm of the Fomori." Lachlan squeezed my arm.

Shen huffed, then began to shoot toward shore. When we neared the city, he turned off the light that shot from his eyes and ducked down low in the water so he couldn't be seen. Our pills had worn off, so he didn't submerge us. If anyone looked, we'd look like a weird pair of synchronized swimmers, shooting through the water way too fast to be normal.

It was strange, zipping through New York City on the back of a Chinese sea dragon, but I couldn't appreciate it. All I could do was worry about my mother. The Protectorate would be actively gathering forces, though, and we'd be back there any moment.

Shen found the first quiet, abandoned spot and swam to the shore, dropping us off.

"Thanks," I said.

He nodded his big head, then dived deep into the river.

I turned to Lachlan. "Can you make a portal?"

He was already doing it. Magic glowed around his palm, and I stepped through the portal, letting the ether suck me in. It pulled me through space and spat me out in Scotland, on the front yard of the castle.

The sun was high in the sky now, midday at least. Lachlan appeared next to me, and we raced into the main entry hall of the castle.

It was chaos inside, full of people in battle garb. More flowed down the stairs and out of the halls, clearly joining the main force that would leave soon.

Oh, thank fates.

Love for the Protectorate slammed into me like a bus. It was my job to hunt the Fates. And the Protectorate would protect anyone who was under attack by them.

But the way that they quickly rallied forces to protect my mother's village made my heart swell. Even Potts stood ready for battle, the old librarian wearing ancient armor and carrying a wicked looking bow and arrow.

"Ana!" Bree raced through the crowd, her boyfriend, Cade, at her side. The massive man towered over her, a scowl on his face. His war face, I had to bet. "Are you okay?"

"Fine."

"You're really wet." She eyed me up and down.

"It's been a long day."

Boris the rat sat on her shoulder, his whiskers twitching angrily. "What are you doing, Boris?"

The rat chittered, but I couldn't understand him. He was clearly pissed, though.

"He's coming to the fight," Bree said. "He's Celtic, remember? I found him in the war camp of the Celtic god Cocidius."

"Thanks for joining the fight, Boris." I had no idea what the little rat would do, but I'd long since stopped doubting someone because of their size or species. *Rat* took that to the extreme, but who was I to judge? I looked at Bree. "Everyone almost here?"

"Ready to go in five minutes."

"No time to change, then."

"I've got you." A voice sounded to my right.

A turned to see Nix, our FireSoul friend from Magic's Bend. And a conjurer.

Joy and gratitude swelled in my chest, threatening to pop

out of my eyes as tears. Cass and Del stood with her, the other two FireSouls who always showed up when we needed them. Three massive men stood behind them. Aidan, Roarke, and Ares, their boyfriends or fiancés or whatever they were. They'd been together years, at least. Connor and Claire, owners of the cafe P & P, stood behind them, grinning.

"Here." Nix shoved some freshly conjured clothes and boots into my arms, then did the same for Lachlan.

"Thank you." I grinned at her, then hurried off to find a quiet place to change. It ended up being a broom cupboard, and I was done in less than a minute.

I rejoined them. "Thank you for coming. We need all the help we can get. I think their forces are at least a hundred highly trained mercenaries."

From the look of our forces here, we had no more than thirty-five or forty. We'd need luck and skill on our side if we weren't going to lose anyone.

"Good, you're back." Jude's voice sounded from behind us.

I turned, glad to see my mentor and hopefully future boss.

"Do you know why they're attacking?" Jude asked.

"No idea. But it was clear that the target was my mother's village."

"All right, we'd better get a move on. We've got as many as we can manage."

I turned, searching for Rowan.

As if she knew what I was looking for, Bree said, "Rowan is getting the buggy."

"Good. That'll help." My fingers itched to take the wheel. I always felt best when fighting from the buggy.

"Time to go!" Jude shouted. "Meet on the lawn! Emily will make a portal!"

We trooped out onto the lawn, ready to fight. Mayhem, the

ghostly pug, flew ahead of everyone, leading the charge with an excited yip.

A massive portal waited for us, glowing bright despite the daylight. Emily, the transport mage, stood next to her creation. It was rare that she made one of these, but this time, we needed it.

Rowan waited with the buggy. Its engine idled with a fierce grumbling sound. I sprinted toward her, then leaped up onto the front platform. Lachlan joined me, along with Bree and Cade. Caro, Ali, and Haris climbed onto the back, while the FireSouls and their partners squeezed in wherever they could fit. Claire and Connor completed the group. We were like a deadly clown car.

From the ground, Jude met my eyes. "We'll save your mom."

My throat tightened. "Thanks."

"Go!" Jude shouted.

Rowan pressed her foot to the gas, and the buggy rolled through the portal, leading the charge toward war.

The ether sucked us in and spat us out in the middle of the same field where I'd gone with Maira and the druids so recently. Slowly, Rowan drove toward the towering stone circle, our fellow fighters marching alongside.

We had to get everyone through, which would be no easy task, since a non-Celt would have to be holding a Celt's hand to make the journey.

I looked over at Cade, who stood with an arm wrapped around Bree's waist. He was Belatucadros, a Celtic war god. "Do you think this will work?"

"We'll try. If everyone holds hands, we might manage it in one group."

"Like a big friendship circle of war." A dry smile tugged at the corner of my lips. "Here's hoping."

I looked at Rowan. "Let everyone get into the circle, but stop the buggy at the edge. I don't want to get sucked through the portal and leave everyone behind."

Once everyone else was inside of the circle, the buggy stopped right at the perimeter.

I stepped up to the edge of the railing on the front fighting platform. I was high enough up that everyone could see me, and all eyes were glued on the buggy. "All right! Join hands."

I reached down, grabbing onto Jude's hand. She reached for Potts, who stood next to her, who reached for Hedy. Jesse Ammons reached for Cade on the other side, and the group of warriors formed a strange parody of something you'd see in a children's schoolyard.

I reached my other hand back for Lachlan, who grabbed it. He then reached for Rowan, and so on, until everyone in the buggy had a hand. Rowan had to turn the steering wheel with a raised knee, but it was no problem.

Finally, we formed a circle.

I shouted, "Get ready!"

Rowan pressed her foot lightly to the gas, and the buggy rolled slowly inside the circle. Immediately, I felt the portal's magic pull at me. I resisted it until the whole buggy was inside. We needed everyone for this.

The tug was difficult to resist, and by the time we were in, I was sweating. I stopped fighting it and let the ether suck me in. I said a quick prayer to the fates—not *those* Fates—then opened my eyes.

We were here.

All of us.

And in the distance, a massive army approached the first exterior wall of the Oppidum.

My heart thundered with the drums of war.

"We're not too late." Gratitude echoed in my voice as I dropped my friend's hands.

"But that's a big army," Bree said.

There were more than one hundred, definitely. Two hundred and fifty. Maybe three hundred.

Thank fates the FireSouls had shown up. They were the big guns, and we needed them.

"I'm going to make room for someone on the buggy." Bree unfurled her silver wings, ready to take to the sky. She called her shield from the ether.

"Be careful." I gave her a hard hug, then she grinned and shot upward.

At the back, Aidan, Cass's boyfriend, stood. "I'm bailing out, too."

"Me too," Cass said.

"Same." Roarke, Del's guy, climbed out.

Magic swirled around them all as they transformed. Roarke's shirt disappeared as his muscles grew and his skin turned a dark gray. Huge wings appeared at his back. Half demon, I'd heard Del call him. He shot toward the sky, ready for an aerial attack.

A swirl of golden light turned Aidan and Cass into huge griffons. Aidan's beak looked like it could chomp a cow in half, and his claws were so wickedly long and sharp that they gave my sword a run for its money. He was a natural griffon shifter, while Cass was a Mirror Mage. Today, she was mirroring Aidan.

It was smart. Aerial attacks would definitely improve our chances.

I turned to the crowd. "Long-range fighters, climb on! We'll drop you off at strategic points."

Three archers climbed on—Potts included—along with two fire mages, an ice mage, and Lavender.

I nodded at her, grateful that she'd come.

She nodded back. "Drop me near some rocks."

"Okay." We might not like each other, but we had each other's backs. That's how the Protectorate worked.

"We'll have to be smart." I looked at Rowan. "Drive to the front of our forces. We'll form a shield for any long-range attacks as we approach."

She grinned and pressed on the gas.

I turned to everyone else and caught Jude's eye. She nodded, giving me the go-ahead.

Steady calm filled me.

I should be nervous.

I'd never commanded such a big operation before. And holy fates, this was big. I'd bet the buggy that no trainee had ever commanded something so enormous.

But this was my fight. My mother. My Otherworld.

The black scar on the land caught my eye, and I vowed to fix it. Somehow.

I turned to the crowd and shouted, "Get behind the buggy! We'll block long-range attacks."

They filed in, and we moved forward. The approaching army was a half mile off, and only a couple hundred yards from the first of the three walls surrounding the Oppidum on the hill.

We moved fast, gaining on them. It helped that Bree flew to the front of their forces and sent her lightning flying into the ground, creating a wall. It scattered them, making them move more slowly. There was something huge in the middle of their forces, almost the size of an elephant.

When the first long-range attack came, I called on my shield magic. It burst forth, as if all my practice lately had helped. Or maybe it was the stakes.

Never had so many lives depended upon me.

The fireball that hurtled toward us slammed into my shield, making my arms shake. We plowed forward, dropping archers and long-range fighters on rock outcroppings that gave them a good vantage point.

"Thanks," I said to Potts as he jumped off.

"Don't think this means I'll let you mess around in the library," he grumbled as he took a knee and began to fire flaming arrows into the crowd of demons that marched toward the walls. He was a crack shot, and his arrows could go insanely far.

"'Course not," I said.

Bree peeled away, and we dropped the rest off. We were close enough now that our fighters split off, headed for the back of the army.

"See you later!" Del shouted from the back of the buggy. She jumped off, her form turning transparent blue as she became half Phantom.

She was the only one of her kind, and damned if she wasn't a sight to behold. She sprinted into the middle of the mercenary army, her sword flying. Nothing could hurt her while she was in her Phantom form, and she'd turn corporeal just long enough for her sword to turn to steel so she cut could off an enemy head. It was a terrifying dance.

Ares kissed Nix, then jumped off next, the vampire hybrid so fast that he almost disappeared as he raced toward the opposing forces.

Ali and Haris jumped off as well, racing toward the closest mercenaries. The djinns disappeared right into the mercenaries, who immediately started to fight each other to the death.

Lachlan turned to me. "I've got to go. Be careful."

I pressed a hard, fast kiss to his lips. "I will. You too."

He jumped off the buggy and shifted into his lion form, then roared as he thundered toward the opposing forces.

Connor joined me on the front platform, while Claire stayed in the middle.

That left us with Rowan behind the wheel and Caro and Nix on the back platform.

"Let's kick demon ass!" Caro shouted.

I grinned.

In the sky, Bree shot her lightning, while the two griffons swooped and dived, taking out four demons at a time as they plowed through the opposing forces. Roarke was just as deadly, his huge wings carrying him down toward the army as his sword glinted in the sunlight. The rest of our friends fought with sword and bow, fire and ice. Magic flew through the air.

I looked for the Fates but couldn't find them. Nor could I feel them. Where were they? At the front?

My eye zeroed in on the massive shape that lumbered along at the front of the pack. It looked like an elephant, but dark magic swirled around it, smelling of rotten fruit and decay. It was some kind of creature built of dark magic—not a living creature at all. It picked up speed as it plowed toward the main gate on the external wall.

It wasn't far off, either.

Four demons rode on top of it, directing it toward its target.

I pointed toward it. "We've got to take it out before it breaks down the wall!"

"Hold on!" Rowan shouted as she pressed her foot on the gas. The buggy jumped forward, and the wind tore at my hair.

This was *exactly* what I liked.

I whooped as we raced forward, catching sight of Princess Snowflake III and Bojangles racing toward the army from the left. Bojangles disappeared, and I pitied the demons that he latched onto. Muffin was nowhere to be seen.

We were close enough to the dark magic beast to launch an attack. I called upon my fire magic, shooting a bolt straight at the creature. It slammed into his side, but he didn't move. I tried again.

No luck.

I sent the next bolt at the demon who rode on the front of the monster. It slammed into him, throwing him off. He was swallowed by the foot soldiers below. Caro shot a jet of water and blasted another demon off, while Connor took out the last two with his potion bombs.

"We need to get closer to get the creature!" I shouted.

Rowan steered the buggy closer. Several mercenaries caught sight of us and veered off, ready to attack. One shot a bolt of green light at us, but Rowan dodged, swerving the vehicle left. The next leapt up with his sword, determined to board.

Claire met him head-on, swinging her blade like the pro she was. She took off his head in one swoop.

Lightning peppered the air from Bree in the sky, taking out demon after demon, while my friends launched land attacks from all sides. We'd taken out half their forces already, but they were so close to the first gate. With that magical elephant plowing along, they were going to breach it.

Then there were only two more walls left.

I directed another blast of fire at the elephant, but it was deflected by the monster's thick hide. Whatever dark magic had created this battering ram of a beast, it was strong. Caro tried another jet of water, this one moving as fast as a bullet.

It, too, bounced off the elephant, and I cursed. Connor tried his potion bombs, but to no avail.

The elephant was nearly there!

I tried calling upon my earth magic, heaving the ground in front of the monster upward. It worked, the ground rising up, but the creature kept running, stumbling over the earth like it was some kind of ramp.

It charged faster, flying off the ramp and into the gate, breaking it.

Shit.

The mercenaries plowed through, into the first ring of land. It was only fifty yards wide. We'd have to stop them before they breached the second gate, which was manned by four Celtic warriors.

Because the Oppidum and the walls were built on a hill, I could see what was happening inside the first ring even though I wasn't in there yet.

The guards on the wall shouted and shot blasts of fire at the oncoming demons, taking out some of them, but there were too many. Our forces had to make it past the wall.

"Clear the way with the buggy!" I shouted.

Rowan jerked the wheel right, plowing into the enemy fighters. We'd run them over, making a clear path for our friends to follow. The massive metal spikes on the sides of the buggy were painted with Ravener poison. Wherever it hit the demons, they froze and fell, the poison deadly.

But there were so many Fomori. The whole place stank of rotten fish and dark magic. They turned and jumped, trying to climb the front of the buggy. I drew my sword and fought them off, side by side with Claire.

When a massive boulder flew in front of the buggy and smashed away most of the demons, I grinned. Another came, flying from the same side and clearing more of the way.

I looked back, catching sight of Lavender, hurling boulders at our enemies, making a path.

"Connor!" Nix shouted from the back platform. "Come help me! I've got an idea!"

Connor climbed back, scrambling over the seats as Rowan kept driving toward the gap in the wall, clearing a path with the buggy.

In the back, Nix's magic swelled on the air. I peeked, catching sight of a massive metal ball attached to chain. She and Connor hooked it off to the back platform and chucked it overboard. The ball bounced in the dirt, slamming into the demons who were closing in behind us.

"Swerve the buggy!" Nix shouted.

Rowan whooped and did as she said, jerking the wheel left and right. The iron ball hanging off the back began to swing wildly, slamming into demons and taking them out.

We cleared a path, and our fellow fighters fell in.

I still couldn't find the Fates, or Muffin. Where the heck were they? The Fates wouldn't miss their own battle. And Muffin wouldn't want to miss *any* battle.

Rowan drove the buggy through the gap in the wall, and I zeroed in on the monster who was racing toward the next gate. He was almost there.

I called upon the earth, making it heave upward, but I was too late. The monster plowed on, breaking through the second wall.

Only one left.

"Faster!" I screamed.

With fewer Fomori in our way, we sped across the hill, climbing upward to the second wall and the gap that the monster had made.

As soon as we drove through, I gave it everything I had, calling upon the earth and commanding it to my will. The ground rose up in front of the monster, a wall of dirt that crashed down on it, sending it rolling backward down the hill.

Rowan swerved right, avoiding the tumbling creature, and the metal ball hanging off the back swung wildly outward, wiping out a few demons in the process. I turned to watch the monster's backward progress.

Lachlan leapt through the gate, his massive lion form even more terrifying in battle. He leapt onto the elephant, and the griffons joined him.

They tore at the creature, and it burst into a cloud of black dust, the magic dissipating. All around, the battle was fading.

Celtic warriors who had guarded the last wall had joined the fray, but most of the battle was over.

My army—my friends—were taking care of the last of the figures.

But the Fates were still nowhere to be seen.

A shiver raced over my spine.

Something was wrong.

In the distance, a tiny shape flew toward me. I squinted.

"Muffin!"

He hurtled toward me, green eyes wide. Boris rode on his back, the little rat waving his tiny arms and squeaking like mad.

"Oh, shit. Something is wrong," Claire said.

Muffin slowed as he neared me, his face wrinkled up with worry. Boris squeaked like his tail was on fire.

Muffin meowed. *Fates invaded from the back of the village. Snuck in with help while everyone was distracted. In the potion master's house. Go!*

16

Panicked, I turned back. "Rowan, drive for the main gates! Fates attacking from the back of the village!"

Rowan pressed on the gas, and the buggy jumped for the last gate.

I waved at the people standing on the wall and screamed, "Let us in! Attack from behind!"

"What? Battle is still going!" An old druid shouted.

Holy crap, was he for real?

I looked for my mother but couldn't see her. "I'm on your side. Come on! Open the gates."

"What?" he shouted.

He couldn't hear me.

They couldn't hear me. Not through the shouts and screams, the clashing of swords.

I turned back to Rowan. "Can you ram it?"

"I can try. Bail out, though. You got no seatbelts."

"Safety first." I jumped off the buggy, followed by Claire, Connor, and Nix, who took a moment to unlatch the metal chain and ball.

I caught Rowan's eye. "Be careful."

She nodded, then turned forward, a determined glint in her eyes. She pressed the gas, and the buggy revved forward, crashing into the wooden gate and slamming through. I saw her jerk forward, her body stopped by the racing-grade safety harness.

A low growl sounded from my side, and I turned. Lachlan stood next to me. I jumped onto his back, and he plowed forward, then jumped through a hole in the fence.

"Wait for me!" Rowan sounded so pissed and determined that Lachlan stopped, waiting.

She scrambled on behind me, grabbing onto my waist.

"Go!" I shouted.

Lachlan leapt forward, sprinting through the village toward the back. Muffin and Boris flew ahead of us, leading the charge. Thank fates for Muffin, finding the Fates.

We sped past shocked faces, but in the air above, I spotted Bree. She hadn't let us out of her line of sight, and now she was backup.

At the far end of the village, we found the potion maker's house. It sat right up against the wall, in a remote corner of town.

They must still be in there! Muffin meowed. *Doing something!*

Boris screeched his rage. Something was *really* pissing off that rat.

A half second later, a crazy old crone lunged out of the house, her wild hair askew. A total rat's nest. Boris started to squeak even louder.

Her eyes widened and she hissed. "Boris!"

I swore Boris screeched, *You bitch!*

Yeah, there was history there. And this must have been the contact who had helped the Fates sneak in. Whatever they'd wanted in the potion master's house, they'd had plenty of time to find it, what with everyone being distracted by the massive attack from the other side of town.

Then the Fates came out, the three shadowy figures looking almost human again, if you ignored the shadowy gray skin and semi-transparent figures.

They had no thread or scissors with them, like the traditional Fates, and were still dressed in their military garb. Something had changed for them, that was for sure. They were playing a different game than they ever had before.

A vision flashed in my mind, so fierce and strong that I couldn't stop it.

My druid sense going wild?

But one of the Fates was looking at me, her eyes burning into mine.

They had lost their thread and scissors. Or someone had taken it away from them. Yes, that was it. I could see it in my mind's eye. It had happened long ago, when they were still old crones dressed in their feminine Roman garb. They lost their power over life and death. Their only power.

They *hated* that.

They wanted to fix it.

So they were.

Right now.

"Ana!" Rowan shouted.

I snapped back to reality, blinking.

The Fates were trapped between us and the building, with the exterior wall at their backs. And damned if they didn't want to escape. It vibrated off of them. The one on the left, the tallest one, had something clutched in her hands.

She couldn't have it.

I called upon my magic, blasting them with flame. It plowed through them, not having any effect.

Bree shot her lightning, but it did no good either.

At my side, Lachlan shifted back to his human form. He called upon the earth, making it rise up. I joined him, adding my magic to his. It slammed into the Fates, and they stumbled back.

Then their magic burst forward, that same terrible sonic boom that had slammed into me before, back in Italy. It tore through my middle, making my organs vibrate. I spun head over heels, tumbling backward, Lachlan at my side. He must have been hit, too.

I slammed into the ground, blinking.

Get up! Muffin screeched.

I heaved myself up, catching sight of the old crone running away. She wasn't my problem.

It was the other two Fates who were running that made my heart thud. The one with the package was already ten feet away. Fifteen.

A scream sounded from the other side.

Your sister! Muffin shrieked.

His tone made a cold shiver run over me.

I turned.

Somehow, Rowan had missed their sonic boom and grabbed ahold of one of the fates, determined to stop her. And instead of blasting her backward, the Fate had grabbed onto her, too, squeezing around her neck.

Rowan kicked and thrashed, trying to break free. She was gasping raggedly, clearly still unable to breathe.

Her face was turning a dark gray. The Fate was killing her. Whatever dark magic she was using was sucking the life right out of Rowan.

Two of the Fates were getting away—with whatever they'd come here for—but there was no choice here.

I raced for Rowan.

Behind me, Lachlan thundered toward the Fates, charging after them. *Please catch them.*

I reached for the Fate who had Rowan, but as soon as my hands hit her, darkness seeped into me. Sickness and death and misery.

I stumbled back, my mind alight.

This was the opposite of me. The opposite of my light magic.

It was so obvious I wanted to cry with joy, but instead, I called on the last of my magic. So much of it was gone, used up in all the fighting we'd been doing. But there was enough. There had to be.

Lightning struck in the background, no doubt from Bree as she tried to stop the other Fates, but I had eyes only for Rowan, who was turning a darker gray every moment.

I let my magic fill me, remembering Sulis. The light burst out of me, so bright it was blinding. It slammed into the Fate, who shrieked and fell backward.

I hit her harder, giving it everything I had. Pouring all the goodness and light and hope into her. She screamed again, then disappeared in a poof of dust.

I stumbled. The light faded.

Rowan gasped, and I ran to her. "Are you okay?"

She nodded, her color returning, and her gaze darted around me, toward where the Fates had run.

They were gone, disappeared through a back gate. In the sky, Bree screamed, a sound so frustrated, I'd never heard anything like it.

"They got away," I said.

Rowan coughed. "Clearly. Bree sounds pissed."

I hugged her. "Are you really okay?"

"Yeah." Her voice was scratchy. "Thought I was a goner for a moment, but I'm fine."

I pulled back and inspected her. She really did look okay. Pale and miserable, but whole and no longer gray. At her side, a pile of dust sat on the ground.

I nudged it with my foot. "I think I killed one."

"Yeah, she sure didn't like your light power."

"Good job, grabbing her."

"Their boom missed me. I thought I was helping." Distress gleamed in her eyes. "You could have gone after the one with the package if not for me."

"No way to know how it would have gone down," I said. "We did our best."

We did our best worked better for kindergartners who were trying to build a sand castle that kept falling down, but I was going to cling to it. And to our victory. I wanted to get back to the main part of the village and check on our forces. Our mother.

I prayed there were no fatalities.

Muffin fluttered next to me, an angry-looking Boris riding on his back.

"What's his deal?" I asked.

The crone was his old master. He's not a fan.

"We'll stop her," I said.

Bree flew overhead and landed next to me. "Lost them. They made it outside the gates to where a portal was waiting. Lachlan tried to grab them but couldn't. They were too fast."

Lachlan padded up to me in his lion form, his big brow creased, frustration evident. He shifted back to human. "I'm sorry I missed them."

I squeezed his arm. "You'll get another chance. There's no way this is over. Not yet."

After the battle—during which we experienced some horrible injuries but no casualties, thank fates—the reunion with my mother and sisters was pretty much the best moment of my life.

The surprise and joy on their faces was something I'd never

forget. Jude had taken a moment to update me on our status and to tell me I'd done a good job, but then she'd left me with my family.

I shot her one last grateful glance as she walked away. While my sisters caught up with our mother, I thanked the FireSouls and their guys. They all looked dirty and beat-up, with blood—both theirs and others—coating their clothes and faces, but everyone was smiling.

"Well done, Ana," Cass said. "You're really coming up in the world."

Absentmindedly, I touched the tattoo at my neck. "I guess I am."

Nix hugged me. "I like your truck. Need to upgrade my collection and do something similar."

I grinned at her, remembering her car collection. "I'll help you."

Del squeezed my arm. "You've got a cool place here. And I'm glad you found your mom."

I smiled at her. "Thanks."

We said our goodbyes, then Connor and Claire came over to say farewell, along with Ali, Haris, and Caro, who made me promise to meet them at the Whiskey and Warlock the next day.

I smiled. "Will do. I promise."

They grinned. "See you."

I owed everyone a big thank you when this was over, but for now, I wanted to be with my mom and sisters. Lachlan hovered at the side, along with Muffin and Boris, who had calmed down considerably now that Hans had found him and given him a tiny juice box.

"Thanks for fighting, Hans," I said. "I didn't know you did that."

"My baguettes are very hard." He made swiping motions

with his hands, like he was using imaginary baguettes for swords.

I laughed and eyed the real sword sheathed at his waist but went along with his joke.

"Come here," my mother said. She had her arms wrapped around each of my sisters, and my eyes prickled.

I joined them for a hug, so happy I thought I would explode into a million pieces and float away.

This was *real*.

Whatever had happened in the past, all the terrible things we'd been through, we were together and alive. Sort of. Alive enough for me, especially considering the fact that we could visit Otherworld and see our mother.

I was pulling back to say that when a heavy jolt of power hit the air. It rumbled through me, strong and fierce.

Sulis.

I knew without looking that she was here.

I pulled away from my mom and sisters and turned. The glowing goddess stood a few feet away from me, her gaze trained on my face. "Well done, Ana."

"Thanks."

"It seems that you are more than worthy of your title, Warrior Druid. The dragons and the Celtic gods chose well."

I smiled. "We're not done yet. The Fates got away."

"You will catch them. In the meantime, I was hoping that you could help me with something."

I felt like I could probably only take a few more steps without falling onto my face with exhaustion, but I nodded. "Sure."

"Together, we will get rid of the poison that they left behind."

"I don't have much magic left." Almost none, in fact. I needed an eight-hour nap and a whole lot of food.

"It is enough."

I nodded and followed her. My family and Lachlan trailed behind, with Muffin fluttering along at my side. Bojangles and Princess Snowflake III joined us. As usual, the white Persian was covered with blood and looked so damned happy. She loved a good battle.

Sulis led us to the closest scar on the land. It stretched across the field, reaching into the distance.

"Now that this is over and they are gone, we can fix the damage that they left behind," she said.

I nodded and took the hand that she held out. Immediately, her magic flowed through me, warming me and giving me strength. It made it easier to call upon the light within me.

Without a doubt, this was my strongest power. *This* was what made me The Druid—Sulis's gift. The rest were valuable and strong, but this was what I was all about. Light and life and health.

She didn't need to give me any instructions. I reached into myself and grabbed the light, then poured it out of me and into the earth. Sulis's touch acted as an accelerant, lighter fluid to my flame.

The magic streaked along the ground, driving away the dark shadow. It zipped across the earth, leaving healthy ground behind. On and on it went, into the distance until we could no longer see it.

But I could feel it, racing over Otherworld and healing the land. After a while—minutes or hours, I had no idea—it stopped.

Everything felt good. Healthy.

I let go of Sulis's hand. "I think we're done."

"I think so, too." She stepped back and smiled. "Well done, Ana."

I grinned at her, and she disappeared.

My mother and sisters stood off to the side, watching me. But Lachlan was at my side.

I turned to him. "Thank you. For everything."

"Of course."

"I don't think this is over."

"I'm sure it's not. But together, we'll stop them. Whatever they took from here, we will get it back."

I reached for him, then pulled him close and rested my head against his chest. "We will. But first I need a nap."

"You've earned it." He shuddered slightly and wrapped his arms around me, pulling me into his embrace.

"What was that about?" I asked.

"For a moment there, I thought you were gone." His voice was rough with emotion. "When I lost sight of you in the battle, I thought my worst fear had come true."

"Losing me is your worst fear?" I looked up at him, shocked.

"According to the Phantoms, it is."

"That's what they were making you feel?"

He nodded.

"Me too." I hugged him tight. "Losing my sisters. My mother. Losing you."

"I'm in good company," he murmured against my head.

"I'm glad we're not pretending anymore."

"Me too."

"Never again," I said. "Never again."

Together, we'd take down the Fates. There were two of them and two of us. And those poor bastards didn't have backup like I did.

I looked toward my family, grateful for everything that I had. For everything that I would have, when we finished this job and stopped the Fates.

Because it would happen. I'd see to it.

Book 4 will be out in July. Continue the adventure now with the free novella, *Death Valley Magic,* that stars the Dragon Gods in their early days, fighting their way across Death Valley. Click here to join my mailing list and get the book, or turn the page for an excerpt.

THANK YOU FOR READING!

I hope you enjoyed Ana's first book as much as I enjoyed writing it. Reviews are *so* helpful to authors. If you want to leave one, you can do so on Amazon.

Join my mailing list to stay updated. You'll also get a free copy of *Death Valley Magic*, the story of the Dragon Gods' early adventures. Turn the page for an excerpt.

EXCERPT OF DEATH VALLEY MAGIC

Death Valley Junction
  Eight years before the events in Undercover Magic

Getting fired sucked. Especially when it was from a place as crappy as the Death's Door Saloon.

"Don't let the door hit you on the way out," my ex-boss said.

"Screw you, Don." I flipped him the bird and strode out into the sunlight that never gave Death Valley a break.

The door slammed behind me as I shoved on my sunglasses and stomped down the boardwalk with my hands stuffed in my pockets.

What was I going to tell my sisters? We *needed* this job.

There were roughly zero freaking jobs available in this postage stamp town, and I'd just given one up because I wouldn't let the old timers pinch me on the butt when I brought them their beer.

Good going, Ana.

I kicked the dust on the ground and quickened my pace toward home, wondering if Bree and Rowan had heard from Uncle Joe yet. He wasn't blood family—we had none of that left besides each other—but he was the closest thing to it and he'd been missing for three days.

Three days was a lifetime when you were crossing Death Valley. Uncle Joe made the perilous trip about once a month, delivering outlaws to Hider's Haven. It was a dangerous trip on the best of days. But he should have been back by now.

Worry tugged at me as I made the short walk home. Death Valley Junction was a nothing town in the middle of Death Valley, the only all-supernatural city for hundreds of miles. It looked like it was right out of the old west, with low-slung wooden buildings, swinging saloon doors, and boardwalks stretching along the dirt roads.

Our house was at the end of town, a ramshackle thing that had last been repaired in the 1950s. As usual, Bree and Rowan were outside, working on the buggy. The buggy was a monster truck, the type of vehicle used to cross the valley, and it was our pride and joy.

Bree's sturdy boots stuck out from underneath the front of the truck, and Rowan was at the side, painting Ravener poison onto the spikes that protruded from the doors.

"Hey, guys."

Rowan turned. Confusion flashed in her green eyes, and she shoved her black hair back from her cheek. "Oh hell. What happened?"

"Fired." I looked down. "Sorry."

Bree rolled out from under the car. Her dark hair glinted in the sun as she stood, and grease dotted her skin where it was revealed by the strappy brown leather top she wore. We all wore the same style, since it was suited to the climate.

She squinted up at me. "I told you that you should have left that job a long time ago."

"I know. But we needed the money to get the buggy up and running."

She shook her head. "Always the practical one."

"I'll take that as a compliment. Any word from Uncle Joe?"

"Nope." Bree flicked the little crystal she wore around her neck. "He still hasn't activated his panic charm, but he should have been home days ago."

Worry clutched in my stomach. "What if he's wounded and can't activate the charm?"

Months ago, we'd forced him to start wearing the charm. He'd refused initially, saying it didn't matter if we knew he was in trouble. It was too dangerous for us to cross the valley to get him.

But that meant just leaving him. And that was crap, obviously.

We might be young, but we were tough. And we had the buggy. True, we'd never made a trip across, and the truck was only now in working order. But we were gearing up for it. We wanted to join Uncle Joe in the business of transporting outlaws across the valley to Hider's Haven.

He was the only one in the whole town brave enough to make the trip, but he was getting old and we wanted to take over for him. The pay was good. Even better, I wouldn't have to let anyone pinch me on the butt.

There weren't a lot of jobs for girls on the run. We could only be paid under the table, which made it hard.

"Even if he was wounded, Uncle Joe would find a way to activate the charm," Bree said.

As if he'd heard her, the charm around Bree's neck lit up, golden and bright.

She looked down, eyes widening. "Holy fates."

Panic sliced through me. My gaze met hers, then darted to Rowan's. Worry glinted in both their eyes.

"We have to go," Rowan said.

I nodded, my mind racing. This was *real*. We'd only ever

talked about crossing the valley. Planned and planned and planned.

But this was *go time*.

"Is the buggy ready?" I asked.

"As ready as it'll ever be," Rowan said.

My gaze traced over it. The truck was a hulking beast, with huge, sturdy tires and platforms built over the front hood and the back. We'd only ever heard stories of the monsters out in Death Valley, but we needed a place from which to fight them and the platforms should do the job. The huge spikes on the sides would help, but we'd be responsible for fending off most of the monsters.

All of the cars in Death Valley Junction looked like something out of *Mad Max*, but ours was one of the few that had been built to cross the valley.

At least, we hoped it could cross.

We had some magic to help us out, at least. I could create shields, Bree could shoot sonic booms, and Rowan could move things with her mind.

Rowan's gaze drifted to the sun that was high in the sky. "Not the best time to go, but I don't see how we have a choice."

I nodded. No one wanted to cross the valley in the day. According to Uncle Joe, it was the most dangerous of all. But things must be really bad if he'd pressed the button now.

He was probably hoping we were smart enough to wait to cross.

We weren't.

"Let's get dressed and go." I hurried up the creaky front steps and into the ramshackle house.

It didn't take long to dig through my meager possessions and find the leather pants and strappy top that would be my fight wear for out in the valley. It was too hot for anything more, though night would bring the cold.

Daggers were my preferred weapon—mostly since they were cheaper than swords and I had good aim with anything small and pointy. I shoved as many as I could into the little pockets built into the outside of my boots and pants. A small duffel full of daggers completed my arsenal.

I grabbed a leather jacket and the sand goggles that I'd gotten second hand, then ran out of the room. I nearly collided with Bree, whose blue eyes were bright with worry.

"We can do this," I said.

She nodded. "You're right. It's been our plan all along."

I swallowed hard, mind racing with all the things that could go wrong. The valley was full of monsters and dangerous challenges—and according to Uncle Joe, they changed every day. We had no idea what would be coming at us, but we couldn't turn back.

Not with Uncle Joe on the other side.

We swung by the kitchen to grab jugs of water and some food, then hurried out of the house. Rowan was already in the driver's seat, ready to go. Her sand goggles were pushed up on her head, and her leather top looked like armor.

"Get a move on!" she shouted.

I raced to the truck and scrambled up onto the back platform. Though I could open the side door, I was still wary of the Ravener poison Rowan had painted onto the spikes. It would paralyze me for twenty-four hours, and that was the last thing we needed.

Bree scrambled up to join me, and we tossed the supplies onto the floorboard of the back seat, then joined Rowan in the front, sitting on the long bench.

She cranked the engine, which grumbled and roared, then pulled away from the house.

"Holy crap, it's happening." Excitement and fear shivered across my skin.

Worry was a familiar foe. I'd been worried my whole life. Worried about hiding from the unknown people who hunted us. Worried about paying the bills. Worried about my sisters. But it'd never done me any good. So I shoved aside my fear for Uncle Joe and focused on what was ahead.

The wind tore through my hair as Rowan drove away from Death Valley Junction, cutting across the desert floor as the sun blazed down. I shielded my eyes, scouting the mountains ahead. The range rose tall, cast in shadows of gray and beige.

Bree pointed to a path that had been worn through the scrubby ground. "Try here!"

Rowan turned right, and the buggy cut toward the mountains. There was a parallel valley—the *real* Death Valley— that only supernaturals could access. That was what we had to cross.

Rowan drove straight for one of the shallower inclines, slowing the buggy as it climbed up the mountain. The big tires dug into the ground, and I prayed they'd hold up. We'd built most of the buggy from secondhand stuff, and there was no telling what was going to give out first.

The three of us leaned forward as we neared the top, and I swore I could hear our heartbeats pounding in unison. When we crested the ridge and spotted the valley spread out below us, my breath caught.

It was beautiful. And terrifying. The long valley had to be at least a hundred miles long and several miles wide. Different colors swirled across the ground, looking like they simmered with heat.

Danger cloaked the place, dark magic that made my skin crawl.

"Welcome to hell," Bree muttered.

"I kinda like it," I said. "It's terrifying but..."

"Awesome," Rowan said.

"You are both nuts," Bree said. "Now drive us down there. I'm ready to fight some monsters."

Rowan saluted and pulled the buggy over the mountain ridge, then navigated her way down the mountainside.

"I wonder what will hit us first?" My heart raced at the thought.

"Could be anything," Bree said. "Bad Water has monsters, kaleidoscope dunes has all kinds of crazy shit, and the arches could be trouble."

We were at least a hundred miles from Hider's Haven, though Uncle Joe said the distances could change sometimes. Anything could come at us in that amount of time.

Rowan pulled the buggy onto the flat ground.

"I'll take the back." I undid my seatbelt and scrambled up onto the back platform.

Bree climbed onto the front platform, carrying her sword.

"Hang on tight!" Rowan cried.

I gripped the safety railing that we'd installed on the back platform and crouched to keep my balance. She hit the gas, and the buggy jumped forward.

Rowan laughed like a loon and drove us straight into hell.

Up ahead, the ground shimmered in the sun, glowing silver.

"What do you think that is?" Rowan called.

"I don't know," I shouted. "Go around!"

She turned left, trying to cut around the reflective ground, but the silver just extended into our path, growing wider and wider. Death Valley moving to accommodate us.

Moving to trap us.

Then the silver raced toward us, stretching across the ground.

There was no way around.

"You're going to have to drive over it!" I shouted.

She hit the gas harder, and the buggy sped up. The reflective surface glinted in the sun, and as the tires passed over it, water kicked up from the wheels.

"It's the Bad Water!" I cried.

The old salt lake was sometimes dried up, sometimes not. But it wasn't supposed to be deep. Six inches, max. Right?

Please be right, Uncle Joe.

Rowan sped over the water, the buggy's tires sending up silver spray that sparkled in the sunlight. It smelled like rotten eggs, and I gagged, then breathed shallowly through my mouth.

Magic always had a signature—taste, smell, sound. Something that lit up one of the five senses. Maybe more.

And a rotten egg stink was bad news. That meant dark magic.

Tension fizzed across my skin as we drove through the Bad Water. On either side of the car, water sprayed up from the wheels in a dazzling display that belied the danger of the situation. By the time the explosion came, I was strung so tight that I almost leapt off the platform.

The monster was as wide as the buggy, but so long that I couldn't see where it began or ended. It was a massive sea creature with fangs as long as my arm and brilliant blue eyes. Silver scales were the same color as the water, which was still only six inches deep, thank fates.

Magic propelled the monster, who circled our vehicle, his body glinting in the sun. He had to be a hundred feet long, with black wings and claws. He climbed on the ground and leapt into the air, slithering around as he examined us.

"It's the Unhcegila!" Bree cried from the front.

Shit.

Uncle Joe had told us about the Unhcegila—a terrifying water monster from Dakota and Lakota Sioux legends.

Except it was real, as all good legends were. And it occasionally appeared when the Bad Water wasn't dried up. It only needed a few inches to appear.

Looked like it was our lucky day.

My heart thundered as the beast circled, undulating in the air in that signature snakey way. Its eyes pierced me as it waited to strike, and I raised my hands, ready for it.

"Use your shield!" Bree shouted.

"I've got to time it!" I didn't have an endless supply of magic, and wasting it at the beginning of our crossing was a bad idea.

"How do we defeat it?" Rowan cried. "You can't hold it off forever."

My mind raced. Uncle Joe had said something about that. Something...

The creature struck. Light glinted on its fangs, and its breath smelled like week-old garbage as it hurtled toward me.

"Ana!" Rowan cried.

I stifled a gag and called upon my shield magic, envisioning a protective barrier between me and the beast.

It burst from my hands, shining and white. The monster's head slammed into the shield, so hard the collision vibrated up my arms. My magic faltered, weakening.

Damn it.

I wished I had offensive magic—fire, ice, a sonic boom like Bree.

Instead, I was a shield. Destined to react, not act.

The monster reared back and slammed its head against the shield again. It hit with such force that I went to my knees, my arms trembling from the strain of keeping the shield up.

"Drop it so I can hit him!" Bree screamed.

I cut off my magic gratefully, panting. The shield dropped, and Bree's magic swelled on the air, smelling like cedar and sounding like a whistling wind. She hurled her sonic boom, a massive force that smashed into the monster and drove it backward.

The Unhcegila plowed into the water and skidded in the shallows. I scrambled to my feet.

The Unhcegila was fast, rising upward to strike again. My heart thundered as it charged.

Bree threw her sonic boom again. It blasted past me, making my insides vibrate, but the core of it hit the monster, who flew backward again.

It was up a half second later.

"My power isn't working on him!" Bree cried.

No sooner had the words left her mouth than the Unhcegila was up and charging. It moved so fast, plowing toward the front of the buggy where Bree was stationed, I didn't have time to call on my magic.

She struck out with her sword as she dived toward the front seat. The blade sliced the monster's cheek as she flew into the footwell, crashing down next to Rowan. The Unhcegila's head slammed into the bars protecting the front platform, denting them.

The engine roared as Rowan stepped on the gas, and the buggy jumped forward, shaking the Unhcegila off. Stunned, it slipped down into the water.

Bree scrambled up. "I need a freaking shield."

"No kidding," Rowan said. "We'll add it to the list."

I spun to watch the Unhcegila, who was already rising, ready to attack again. I steadied myself on the back platform as we drove away—I was the only thing between it and my sisters.

I'm not going to let it get them.

Its scales glinted in the light, but there was something at its head that shined brighter. A gem—right between its eyes. A tiny red crystal.

A memory flashed in my mind.

"We have to smash the gem!" I cried.

My memory was hazy, but I swore I remembered Uncle Joe telling us the tale of the Unhcegila. Destroying the gem would kill the beast—for now, at least. It would appear again to another traveler, but if we wanted to get it off our butts, we'd have to destroy that gem. And whoever did would get to keep it, and it would bring good luck.

This was going to be up to me. Bree fought with a sword, and Rowan was driving.

I drew a dagger from my boot. The Unhcegila charged, its breath wafting over me, reeking like hot garbage. It opened its mouth wide, fangs glinting.

I hurled my blade, but the monster dodged, then plowed toward me. Before I could build my shield, Bree threw her sonic boom. It blasted past my left shoulder, sending me flying toward the right. I slammed into the safety rails.

The sonic boom nailed the monster right in the face, and the beast tumbled backward.

"Thanks, Bree!" I pushed off the rails and grabbed another dagger.

The monster was rising, but slower this time. Bree's repeated blasts were working. It was weakening.

This was it. My chance.

I used the monster's slowness to my advantage, throwing my dagger right for its eyes. The blade pierced the crystal, and magical energy exploded outward. It blew my hair back from my face and stole the breath from my lungs.

The Unhcegila disappeared in a burst of silver light. A small red crystal flew up into the air, turning end over end and sparkling like a ruby.

"Turn around!" I screamed.

"Why?" Rowan shouted.

"Because!"

"Great reason!" Rowan yanked the wheel to the right, and the buggy made a sharp U-turn. I clung to the railing, keeping my gaze pinned to the crystal. It hurtled back toward the ground, splashing into the water.

The red gem glowed brightly, and I pointed toward it. "Head for the glow!"

Rowan did as I asked, and I climbed over the side of the platform, clinging to the safety railing. "Slow down!"

As we neared the crystal, Rowan slowed the buggy. The gem gleamed brightly, and I hung low, scooping it out of the water. It was warm in my hand, and I squeezed it tight, scrambling back onto the platform.

"Can we keep going now?" Rowan asked.

"Yep!" I looked at the gem briefly. The center was black where my dagger had hit it, but the rest gleamed red and bright. I wasn't sure if it really was lucky, but I could use all the help I could get, so I shoved it into my pocket.

Rowan cut through the rest of the Bad Water without incident, the silver liquid spraying up around the tires and glinting in the sun.

The buggy cut across the desert as the sun beat down upon us. I shielded my eyes, squinting into the distance. Everything was beige, all different shades. And it all shimmered with danger. The air stank with it.

"You smell that?" Rowan asked.

"Yeah, dark magic." It was the thing that made the desert nearly impassable, and the reason that Hider's Haven was so protected. If you wanted to lie low—like, *really* low—that was the place to do it. It was full of criminals, mostly. But also innocent people who were trying to avoid criminals. Get in trouble with the magical mob? Hider's Haven was the supernatural version of witness protection.

Rowan expertly drove the car around scrub brush and boulders. Up ahead, the air shimmered, making it hard to determine what was coming at us. But the air stank with dark magic and prickled, abrading my skin.

Whatever it was, I knew it'd be bad.

~~~

Join my mailing list at www.linseyhal.com/subscribe to continue the adventure and get a free copy of *Death Valley Magic*. No spam and you can leave anytime!

AUTHOR'S NOTE

Thanks for reading *Celtic Magic!* If you've read any of my previous books, you might have noticed that I like to include historical places and mythological elements in my stories. Sometimes the history of these things is so interesting that I want to share more, and I like to do it in the Author's Note instead of the story itself.

There's a lot of mythology and history in *Celtic Magic*, starting with the Kobolds. They are figures from Germanic mythology that have survived into modern times as part of German folklore. They're interesting creatures who can take the shape of a person, animal, fire, or a candle, and they are often invisible. In many cases, they are ambivalent house sprites that perform chores. If they are insulted or neglected, they might play tricks. In some stories, they were so obnoxious that they drove inhabitants from their homes. Annoyingly, they sometimes followed those inhabitants, informing them that they would never leave them alone. In other cases, they'd set up shop in a place and never leave. These are the Kobolds that inspired the ones in *Celtic Magic*.

Now, moving onto Celtic myth. There was a whole of it in

this story. One of the first things that I'd like to note is that the Celts did not build the stone circles that are famous throughout the UK. Most of these were built thousands of years prior by an entirely different culture. The Celts often used the circles for ceremonial purposes, however, and who could blame them? Modern Druids and Pagans still use them today.

The Oppidum where Ana's mother lives is a traditional type of Celtic fortified settlement that was common during the 1st and 2nd centuries BC. They were built from eastern Britain all the way to Spain and Hungary. I debated whether or not to use the word Oppidum for this type of settlement because it is the Latin word, not the Celtic. The Celts certainly had their own name for this type of city. While some Celtic cultures did have written language, not much of it survived. Since we don't know the Celtic word for this type of city, I decided to go with the Roman one.

I'm sure it would annoy some ancient Celts if they found out that I used this term, but it illustrates an interesting point—much of what we know about the Celts comes from the writings of the Romans, one of their greatest enemies. As a result, it can be hard to say what is true in Roman writing. They could have fudged the facts in order to help their own cause (they likely did). For example, the wild Celts could have been used as propaganda, or as a means to increase the size of the Roman army.

The first challenge that Ana faces is at the Iron Age forge, where she must solve the riddle to create a bridge. I'd like to confess to taking some liberties with the nature and construction of this forge. Normally, they were built a little differently, but it didn't work as well for the story. But I wanted to bring in iron production since it was so vital to the Celts, and this seemed like a fun way to do so. Piles of Iron Age slag, the black glass waste that is a byproduct of iron production, can be found all over Europe. Evidence of their iron working is everywhere.

The *Cŵn Annwn,* the spectral hounds of the Welsh Otherworld, are one of my favorite parts of Celtic myth. You may remember them from one of Del's books. I love them so much that I included them here as well. They are often associated with the Wild Hunt, where they chase wrongdoers until they can no longer run. In some stories, they escort souls on their journey to the Otherworld.

The Otherworld is an interesting concept in Celtic religion, primarily because there was no singular type of Otherworld. As I've mentioned before, the Celts were a loose group of people with a similar culture, but they didn't have one religion with the same pantheon of gods. The Irish Celts worshipped different gods than the ancient Celts in Hallstatt, Austria. For the purposes of this story, I created one big Otherworld contains many elements of Celtic culture from all over Europe. Ana has only been to part of the Celtic Otherworld, and while she is there, she encounters a mishmash of Celtic figures. That's one of the most fun things about writing fiction—I get to take the most interesting bits and leave all the rest.

One of those interesting bits is the Kelpie, a horse/man figure who inhabits the lakes of Scotland. Nearly every sizable body of water in Scotland has an associated Kelpie, and they are such an important part of the folklore that there are two modern enormous statues of them along one of the major highway.

It was my invention to make the Kelpie the sworn enemy of the Dullahan, who is an Irish mythological creature similar to the headless horseman. Traditionally, the Dullahn chases those who are about to die. When he (or she) stops their horse and calls out the victim's name, they immediately perish. Obviously, I changed this a bit. The Bean Nighe is a figure from Scotland who is essentially as I represented her, though she cannot turn into a goddess. She is a messenger from the Otherworld, washing the clothes of those about to die.

Sulis is a Romano-Celtic god from Bath, England, where the famous Roman baths are located. She is an example of how Roman and Celtic religion meshed during the Roman occupation of Celtic Britain. She presided over the spring that fed the baths, receiving sacrifices and also requests for vengeance. The archaeological record suggests that people viewed her as both a mother-goddess figure and also one who would exact revenge if you inscribed your request on a clay tablet and left it for her to find. These are known as the curse tablets, and about 130 were found at Bath. They are primarily related to theft and some of them are quite extreme. A famous example is one that reads, "Docimedis has lost two gloves and asks that the thief responsible should lose their minds [sic] and eyes in the goddess' temple."

It seems the Docimedis was really pissed about those gloves.

One of my favorite parts of the book was the riddle at the lake where Ana had to find the correct objects and put them on the flat stone platform. This is meant to represent one of the most famous Celtic sites in the world—La Tène at Lake Neuchâtel in Switzerland. This site is so important that a whole subset of Celtic culture was named after it. The discovery of the site is really cool too.

In 1857, the level of the lake dropped substantially due to drought. Over the course of several decades, historians discovered thousands of weapons, along with the remains of dwellings built on pilings (wooden posts) out in the water. There are several interpretations of the site that try to answer why thousands of weapons were found underwater. I chose the interpretation that they were sacrificial objects.

As Ana was entering the sacred grove, she noticed some pillars inset with skulls. This is a nod to the famous site of Roquepertuse in southern France. The site likely dates from the 5th and 6th centuries BC and contained many amazing Celtic artifacts, including columns that were inset with human skulls. Though this was a bit of a random inclusion in the book, I chose to add it because I wanted to reflect how far and wide Celtic culture spread.

Lastly—Boudica, the warrior who gave Ana her torc. Boudica is my favorite historical figure and an important cultural icon in Britain. She was the brave Celtic warrior queen who rallied her people, the Iceni tribe, to fight against the Roman occupation of Britain in AD 60 and 61. Prior to this, her people had a truce with Rome. After the death of her husband, Rome violated that truce. In one account, they flogged Boudica and raped her daughters.

As a result, Boudica rallied her tribe and several other neighboring Celtic tribes. The Celts were a loose conglomeration of tribal kingdoms at this point and there was no single central leader. They agreed to follow Boudica, however, and what resulted was a campaign across Britain in which Boudica's army successfully destroyed several Roman cities. They were so successful that Rome nearly withdrew from Britain entirely. Boudica might have won the whole war and forced Rome to retreat, but she lost the Battle of Watling Street in AD 61. After this, she either killed herself to avoid capture or died of illness.

It's an amazing story with a crappy ending, if you as me. The first book that I ever wrote, a paranormal romance, told the story of Boudica reincarnated in modern day. She got a second chance to beat the Romans once and for all, and it was very satisfying.

I think that's it for the history and mythology in *Celtic Magic* —at least the big things. I hope you enjoyed the book and will come back for more of Ana, Lachlan, Rowan, and Bree!

ACKNOWLEDGMENTS

Thank you, Ben, for everything. There would be no books without you.

Thank you to Jena O'Connor and Lindsey Loucks for your excellent editing. The book is immensely better because of you! Thank you to Kelly H., Nadine M., Gisela S., Skye M., Lita A., Julie S., Alisa S., and Marina S. for your help with the German.

Thank you to Orina Kafe for the beautiful cover art. Thank you to Collette Markwardt for allowing me to borrow the Pugs of Destruction, who are real dogs named Chaos, Havoc, and Ruckus. They were all adopted from rescue agencies.

GLOSSARY

Alpha Council - There are two governments that enforce law for supernaturals—the Alpha Council and the Order of the Magica. The Alpha Council governs all shifters. They work cooperatively with the Alpha Council when necessary—for example, when capturing FireSouls.

Blood Sorcerer - A type of Magica who can create magic using blood.

Dark Magic - The kind that is meant to harm. It's not necessarily bad, but it often is.

Demons - Often employed to do evil. They live in various hells but can be released upon the earth if you know how to get to them and then get them out. If they are killed on Earth, they are sent back to their hell.

Dragon Sense - A FireSoul's ability to find treasure. It is an internal sense that pulls them toward what they seek. It is easiest to find gold, but they can find anything or anyone that is valued by someone.

Djinn - Possesses invisibility and the ability to possess others for brief periods of time.

Earthwalking Gods - Reincarnates of the ancient gods who

can walk upon the earth. They are mortal but with all the power of that god.

Enchanted Artifacts – Artifacts can be imbued with magic that lasts after the death of the person who put the magic into the artifact (unlike a spell that has not been put into an artifact —these spells disappear after the Magica's death). But magic is not stable. After a period of time—hundreds or thousands of years depending on the circumstance—the magic will degrade. Eventually, it can go bad and cause many problems.

Fire Mage – A mage who can control fire.

FireSoul - A very rare type of Magica who shares a piece of the dragon's soul. They can locate treasure and steal the gifts (powers) of other supernaturals. With practice, they can manipulate the gifts they steal, becoming the strongest of that gift. They are despised and feared. If they are caught, they are thrown in the Prison of Magical Deviants.

The Great Peace - The most powerful piece of magic ever created. It hides magic from the eyes of humans.

Magica - Any supernatural who has the power to create magic—witches, sorcerers, mages. All are governed by the Order of the Magica.

Order of the Magica - There are two governments that enforce law for supernaturals—the Alpha Council and the Order of the Magica. The Order of the Magica govern all Magica. They work cooperatively with the Alpha Council when necessary—for example, when capturing FireSouls.

Seeker - A type of supernatural who can find things. FireSouls often pass off their dragon sense as Seeker power.

Shifter - A supernatural who can turn into an animal. All are governed by the Alpha Council.

Transporter - A type of supernatural who can travel anywhere. Their power is limited and must regenerate after each use.

Undercover Protectorate - A secret organization dedicated to protecting supernaturals and solving the crimes that no one else will.

Vampire - Blood drinking supernaturals with great strength and speed who live in a separate realm.

ABOUT LINSEY

Before becoming a writer, Linsey Hall was a nautical archaeologist who studied shipwrecks from Hawaii and the Yukon to the UK and the Mediterranean. She credits fantasy and historical romances with her love of history and her career as an archaeologist. After a decade of tromping around the globe in search of old bits of stuff that people left lying about, she settled down and started penning her own romance novels. Her Dragon's Gift series draws upon her love of history and the paranormal elements that she can't help but include.

COPYRIGHT